THE

HALLOWEEN LEGION

 A Wild Cat Books Publication

BOOK ONE

THE CREEPY, CRAWLY, CARNIVAL OF CHAOS

by

MARTIN POWELL

For my brothers,
who first showed me the magic of
Halloween.

"The Early Bird and The Thunder Lizard"

"LOUSY WEATHER," Sheriff Dave Ross grumbled, squinting through the veil of mist oozing over his windshield.

"At least the rain stopped," replied Deputy Les Charles with a shrug. "Wonder what's got ol' Monk Whelan so riled up this time?"

The patrol car bounced and squeaked, splashing through the muddy ruts in the gravel road. A cold fog was creeping in from the surrounding hollows, reducing visibility to practically zero. It was a miserable night.

"Said he heard funny noises in the woods behind his fillin' station," the sheriff sniffed. "Probably just a couple trees blowed over from the storm, but we'd better check it out."

"Say, Dave," Les smirked, dribbling stale coffee down his chin. "Maybe it was the wild Goat-Boy."

Sheriff Ross groaned, cussing under his breath.

"Don't start that again."

The deputy knew the subject was a sore point with his boss. He kept on digging deeper.

"Oh, I don't know, Dave. Lots of folks has claimed to see 'im. Half-boy, half-goat. Wild as the devil. Crawlin' on his belly through the cornfields and scratchin' on their window screens at night…"

A deer suddenly leaped in front of the headlights and Dave jammed on the brakes with a rattling skid, barely missing the animal.

"Confound it!" he barked. "Look, for the last time, there ain't no Goat-Boy. If there was, he'd be in my jail."

Deputy Charles grinned. He liked getting the sheriff worked up, especially on long, dull patrols like this one.

"Well, if that's so," Les continued, gleefully, "how'dya explain ol' lady Vowels story of seein' the Goat-Boy in her pond, eatin' up her pet ducks? Or Monk sayin' he saw him tangled up in that barbed wire fence last Easter Sunday, and leavin' behind tar instead of blood on the prongs?"

Sheriff Ross wheeled up to the Early Bird gas station and cut the engine.

"Ol' lady Vowels is older than the hills and Monk was loaded on Wild Turkey again, that's how I explain—"

Dave stopped in mid-sentence, gaping through the clouded windshield. He flicked on the big spotlight and played it slowly over the front of the Early Bird. The center of the structure, from the tin roof to its concrete foundation, had collapsed as if a colossal pile driver had wedged the building into the soggy earth. The sheriff and deputy soberly exited the car, their flashlights knifing through the wormy ribbons of fog.

"What the—?" Les's puff of breath mixed with the mist. "Was it an explosion, or somethin'?"

Dave shook his head, kicking at some of the loose lumber.

"Don't think so. There's no fire. No smoke. Just this dang fog. C'mon, let's find Monk."

Warily, Dave and Les entered the crumpled wreck of the Early Bird as if they were exploring an unknown cavern. It was damp and dripping and strange inside, barely resembling the place they had known for so many years. The beams of their flashlights bounced back from the cracked plaster walls. Mushy comic books and scattered candy bars squashed under their boots with each uneasy step.

"I'm not seein' him," Les muttered, starting to sweat despite the chill.

"Maybe he got out in time," Dave nodded. "Let's look around outside."

They searched the grounds thoroughly, growing nervous at the lack of cricket chatter. The nearby woods were too quiet. It was unnatural, unearthly. Somehow, the whole surrounding three acres of the Early Bird filling station just didn't look right.

"I don't get it," the sheriff finally admitted. "Did an eighteen wheeler crash into the Early Bird? If so, where is it? And there are no tire tracks."

"Might have been a tornado," Les mused, aloud. "Remember last year? Dang thing chewed up half the town."

Sheriff Ross tilted his hat, scratching his head.

"Naw, there weren't no severe weather tonight. Just that short thunderstorm and a little wind. Besides, nothin' else was touched. The sign is still okay. Look for yourself."

Deputy Charles glanced up at the Early Bird sign looming thirty feet above him, and promptly stumbled down into the mud.

"Les—! You alright?"

"Yeah... must've fell in a pothole or... what in tarnation...? Look! There's a whole bunch of 'em!"

A long trail of washtub-sized craters winded its way toward the dark woods.

The sheriff gave his deputy a quick tug, regaining his footing.

"Dave, those things... they're some kind of tracks!"

"You're nuts," Sheriff Ross gritted his teeth. "Your Goat-Boy yarns are startin' to make you goofy. C'mon, let's see if Monk maybe went home before we call in the state boys on this."

Then, they heard it. Both of them. There could be no mistake. Something very big, and alive, was stomping its way out of the wet forest. Hundred year old oaks splintered and fell, shoved aside by massive tons of sinew and scales.

Abruptly, a gleaming reptilian head emerged from the gloom of the wood's edge, followed by an elongated serpentine neck and pillar-like legs propelling the monstrous body relentlessly forward.

Dave reached for his revolver, but found the holster empty.

"Must've dropped my gun somewhere in the car!"

Les grabbed him by the sleeve.

"How many times have I told you that old horse pistol of yours is too big for your holster?! C'mon—the shotguns are in the trunk!"

There wasn't a chance. The lumbering, crushing creature was suddenly upon them like a living locomotive. Each leviathan step shook the soggy ground, spewing up spirals of mud with each deafening impact.

Both men ran blindly, the black bulk of the gigantic beast blotting out the dark grey sky above them. Les was the fastest and suddenly realized Dave wasn't beside him, or behind him. He paused just long enough that the crashing Early Bird sign struck him brutally to the sodden earth.

Struggling to catch his breath, the deputy watched in bleak fascination as the colossal creature thundered past him, hurling gravel in its wake with the fierceness of buckshot. To Les's horror, he could see part of Dave's red-stained uniform fixed under the claws from one of the gargantuan feet, flapping with each terrible step.

Dreamlike, the behemoth plowed on across the road and into a cornfield, vanishing over a hill.

All was quiet again, as the deputy attempted to escape from under the heavy steel post. Only the rain-moistened soil had saved Les from being squashed like a melon, and he knew it. He strained

and tried again. The weighty post wouldn't even budge. Already the mud was oozing inside his collar, pressing against his face. The oppressive weight was burying him alive.

Suddenly, with a groaning creak of ruptured steel, Les was free.

Wiping the slop from his eyes, the deputy witnessed the powerful figure of a very large man standing above him, shrouded in the mist. The stranger must have been all of seven feet tall, or possibly even more. As Les staggered to his feet, the top of his head barely reached the giant's ponderous chest.

"Th-thank you. Don't think nothin's broken," he gasped, "but I must be in shock or somethin'. I thought I just saw a... a dinosaur kill my best friend."

An abrupt flash of lightning illuminated the stranger, revealing his weird garment of midnight black patterned with gleaming, white-painted bones.

"You saw it because that's what happened," the skull-mask nodded. "Sometimes seeing is believing."

And Deputy Charles fainted dead away.

"No More Molly-Pop"

MOLLY SIGHED, rolling her eyes. Her boredom was positively poisonous.

Old Mr. Foley kept droning on from the blackboard about pronouns and dangling participles, alternating his machine-perfect cursive between yellow and white chalk, in a dull as dishwater attempt to be colorful. Molly found it much more interesting to watch a fly climb the drape over the high classroom windows.

She flinched suddenly, bolting up from her desk. Foley blinked at her, fish-eyed behind his thick glasses.

"You have something to contribute, Miss Aldrich?" he asked, vacantly.

Molly flushed red, even at the part in her dark hair. She shook her head and sat down quickly, sinking low. Foley blinked again, then blabbered on, quite unperturbed, his stub of chalk squeaking like a drowsy mouse.

Already an angry little welt was starting to bloom just behind Molly's ear, the result of the projectile paperclip fired from a rubber band. Then, another tiny missile stung her shoulder. She hissed something indecorous under her breath, turned in her seat, and peered fiercely at the sharpshooter.

Bobby Langster sneered back at her, forming a mocking cross with his index fingers. She knew it had been him, even without looking. Molly had a somewhat spooky reputation due to the kind of books she preferred to read and many of the kids teased her constantly, but Bobby Langster was by far the worst of the lot.

As the two glared at each other, Molly's dark chocolate eyes lost their warmth. Oddly, Langster thought he saw tiny penlights of butane blue suddenly spark in her pupils. Merely a trick illusion of the flickering phosphorescent bulbs, no doubt. Even so, Langster shivered secretly, and took to tormenting a different victim.

"Attention, please…" a gravelly voice from the ceiling crackled through the static P.A. speakers. "Molly Aldrich report to Mr. Whitfield's office. That's Molly Aldrich to see Mr. Whitfield."

Molly groaned, gathering up her books. Not the guidance counselor. Again. This was getting to be a monthly ordeal. Still, at least she was escaping old Foley's somnambulistic sermon on semantics, which hummed on as she closed the door more-or-less gratefully behind her.

The empty corridor clacked with her heels echoing off the rows of drab, muck-hued lockers with a steely zing. Molly could glimpse class after class through the slit windows, most everyone inside looking drowsy and disconnected at their desks. What a dismal waste of time and space.

The receptionist frowned at Molly as she clacked past her toward Mr. Whitfield's tiny office. Unfortunately, she knew the path well enough to walk it blindfolded, and the reek of the counselor's mentholated cough drops clearly led the way. She hesitated just outside the open door, taking a deep breath.

Okay, she winced, as a flock of moths fluttered in her belly. Let's get this over with.

Burtrend Whitfield sat with his bony elbows fixed upon his desk, as usual, starched noodle fingers pressed together like a church's steeple. His deep-set onyx stare was almost always fixed at the school calendar on the south wall, and he rarely ever made eye-contact with a student. He'd reminded Molly of a mannequin since the ninth grade.

"Come in, Molly. Close the door, please," Whitfield was always plastically polite.

She took a seat, and skimmed the room briefly. Whitfield had added something to the wall, one of those sorrowful big-eyed kitten prints. The picture disturbingly matched the rest of the otherwise undecorated, cheerless office.

"Now then," he ruffled busily through the thick folder. "I suppose you know what this about?"

"My, um, my grades, I guess," Molly replied, hating how small she always sounded in that office.

Whitfield nodded, gravely.

"They've been slipping again. What do you think the trouble is?"

"I dunno," she shrugged. "Just dumb, maybe."

He rummaged through the documents, the crisp papers crackled like kindling.

"You're a bright girl, Molly. Very impressive I.Q. scores. A touch of laziness, though, I suspect. Yes?"

Molly nodded. The temperature in the cramped office had suddenly, and quite significantly, increased. It was at least ten degrees warmer.

"Yeah, prolly."

"But not too lazy," he rubbed his lack of chin. "For example, I'm delighted that you've seen fit to remain with us till graduation. This seems especially hopeful to me, since you've already accumulated all of your high school credits and yet—"

"Uh, what did you say?" Molly's heart jumped. "I don't understand."

Whitfield removed a monogrammed handkerchief and dabbed at the perspiration accumulating on his long upper lip. The room was growing uncomfortably hot.

"Oh my. You mean you didn't realize?" Whitfield's frown increased, brimming with moisture. "Oh dear. All right, let me see… yes, here it is. Back when you first enrolled here you obtained a physician's note excusing you from gym class, and proceeded to fill that period with a variety of elective courses. Also, you've attended summer school for the past couple years—due to the insistence of your various foster families—and as a result, your total quota of credits for completing high school was accomplished as of last term. Now, I'll admit that completing high school two years early is quite impressive, but that's no excuse for becoming lazy now."

The little office grew steamier. Even the metal top of Whitfield's desk was starting to feel unpleasant to his touch, although, of course, he'd never complain in front of a student. Instead, the guidance counselor merely mopped his dripping grey forehead.

Molly had hardly noticed the heat. The silence was suddenly so intense she could hear the ticking of the wall clock. Surely she must be dreaming.

"You… you mean, I'm done? Done with high school?" she stammered, the words sounded unreal.

"Well, legally speaking, yes. But—where are you going?"

She was already opening the door.

"I'm done. You said it, yourself."

"Wait! There are still opportunities here that—wait! You can't just… you should at least talk this over with your foster family—"

Molly had been on her own since last month, but she didn't need to tell him that. In fact, she didn't need to say another word.

As she'd already said, she was *done*.

The halls looked different now, even clogged and crowded with students rushing and pushing past. Not so forlorn, somehow. Even Molly's old rusty locker wasn't so much like the Pandora's Box as it always had seemed. She quickly grabbed her jacket and pondered the remaining contents of text books, and yesterday's uneaten lunch. This was the last time. What should she take with her? Anything at all?

"Molly! There you are!"

Fortunately, she knew the voice. This was friendly territory.

"Oh. Hi, Miss Hix," Molly grinned sheepishly, suddenly feeling inexplicably guilty.

"The new literary mag is here!" Patricia Hix was positively giddy, handing Molly the magazine. "Your poem is on page twenty-three! Have a look!"

Molly flipped through the pulpy pages. Yup, her poem was there, all right. That was pretty spectacular.

"Wow. Cool. Thanks," was all she could murmur.

The teacher beamed at her.

"I'm so proud of you, Molly. Sorry the mag will be losing you next year. See you at tomorrow's meeting."

No, she wouldn't, Molly mused, watching Miss Hix hurry happily down the hall, waving back at her. Not like the others, Patricia Hix was one of the good ones. Enthusiastic, pretty, looking more like a slightly older sister than a teacher; Molly had liked her from the start. She didn't want to say good-bye. All of the sudden her victory exit darkened a bit. But only a little.

Clasping the magazine, she grinned again, and slammed the locker shut. This was all she needed to take with her. Only this.

"Late for an exorcism, Molly-Pop?" Bobby Langster stood smirking next to the trashcan.

Molly-Pop. She truly, absolutely, positively, detested, hated, and loathed that nickname. Langster had smugly invented it himself, in a moment of imaginary wit. He never let her forget it.

Best to ignore him, Molly supposed, going on her way. A zipping paperclip stung her bottom like a wasp. She whirled around, face flushed. Her tearful eyes had that funny bluish light again.

"That hurt!" she screamed.

"Wasn't supposed to tickle, Molly-Pop" Langster leered, laughing loudly.

Suddenly, a ferocious blast of heat erupted from the trashcan as it burst into orange and red flames.

"Oww! Oww! Oww!" Langster cried, stumbling clumsily, falling on his keys. Already the back of his hand was blistering.

Molly stared, startled and confused. The flames were already dying down in the trash container, weirdly in sync with her plummeting pulse. She reached over and pulled the fire alarm, then turned and walked out the door—bells buzzing behind her—never to return.

Outside on the steps, Molly surveyed her new domain.

"Okay," she breathed, smiling. "Now what?"

And, she started for home.

Molly never thought to glance behind her as a sleek black cat, with a most peculiar shadow, sinisterly stalked her from a distance.

CHAPTER THREE

"The Meandering Ghost of Lonesome Hollow"

"SO WHAT'S it like being sheriff, Les?" Golan Whelan wondered, slogging through the dewy field.

Sheriff Les Charles trudged alongside him, the mud sucking at his boots. It felt colder than it was supposed to be, and his breath puffed like smoke. The slate-colored late afternoon sky threatened more rain, and Lonesome Hollow was not the place to be in a downpour. He quickened their pace.

"Pretty much the same as when I was deputy," Les shrugged a bit awkwardly. "I mean, I'm doin' the same job, just more of it. The county won't pay the tab for more help, so for now I'm getting' use to a lot less sleep."

Golan nodded in sympathy.

"Shame what happened to ol' Dave," he muttered. "We was in the war together, y'know."

"Yeah."

"Kind of a freak thing, huh? Hit and run with that eighteen wheeler smackin' into him like that. Always did say them truckers drove too blamed fast in front of the Early Bird. Never did find Monk, didja? We was cousins you know, growed up together."

"Yeah. I know."

"It's a shame."

"Yeah. It is."

Les felt his gut twist. The weirdness at the Early Bird gas station had been less than a month ago, and its memory still gnawed at him. The guilt of his falsified report could hardly be absolved simply because no one would have believed what had actually happened. He wasn't even quite so sure himself, anymore. It was either do his job, or go to the nuthouse. The conscience-laden choice was simple enough.

"Okay, Golan," Les had to change the subject, "where is this thing you needed to show me?"

Golan Whelan stopped in his tracks. A tough, weathered man. Nothing much ever bothered him, but he was aberrantly anxious now.

"It's down there, deeper in the holler," he pointed to the tangle of woods and weeds at the bottom of the hill.

Clearly, Golan wasn't going any further.

"Alright," Les drew Dave's old Colt from his cramped holster. "I'll be right back. Now, you know these woods and I don't. It'll be gettin' dark soon. Wait for me and we'll walk back to the road together, y'hear?"

The sheriff waited till Golan nodded, then shuffled down the hill. Briars and thistles plucked at the stiff fabric of his new uniform. Les paused for a moment at the forest's edge, huffing out frosty breaths. It was very dark, very quiet in there. A sudden cold spatter of rain forged him forward, into the tangled gloom.

And there it was. The wreck of a house Golan had accidentally discovered while rabbit hunting. A house that wasn't supposed to be there.

Cracked whitewashed slabs glowed in the bough-dimmed twilight like phosphorous. Empty, uneven windows gaped black as pitch. Abruptly, Les recoiled, his teeth chattering. Golan was right, no doubt about it. Someone was moving around inside those old ruins.

Les thumbed back the hammer on the old Colt with a sharp snap, and slowly proceeded forward. Notions of the Goat-Boy bounced around in his brain. Not that Les really believed in those yarns, but lately he'd been witness to much stranger things.

Ridiculous. Moronic. Bull. Probably just an old tramp, that's all. Nothing to get the jitters over. Still, Les's molars clattered to beat the band.

As he got nearer the warped, yawning doorway began to look oddly familiar.

"That's the Fridley house, ain't it, sir?"

Les spun at the soft voice behind him, awkwardly swinging the ponderous pistol. He gawked, blinked, and laughed.

"A bit early for Trick'r Treats," Les chuckled, shaking his head. "What're you doin' playin' way out here?"

The slight figure approached the sheriff shyly, his grass-stained sneakers somehow avoiding the crunch of the fallen leaves. It was a just a kid, probably about ten or eleven years old, draped in a white thread-bare bed sheet. From the hushed, timid voice Les could tell it was a boy.

"S'matter, son? You lost?" Les bent low, grinning.

The shroud shrugged.

"Dunno. Just meanderin', I guess, sir."

Les stood up and took a closer look at the house, paying particular attention to the surrounding trees and underbrush. The sudden truth astonished him, and he let out a low whistle.

"Well, don'tcha fret none, I'll get you home. And you're right about this bein' the Fridley's farmhouse, or at least that's what it used to be," he peeked into the door, but didn't enter. "Used to play checkers with ol' Fred Fridley on what's left of this porch. Yessiree, spent many a fine summer evening here. Poor ol' Fred."

Continuing his survey, poking his head in a couple of the broken windows, Les rambled on.

"Yup, I reckon that dat-blasted freak tornado from last autumn must've tossed this whole house a full two or three miles into these here woods. I've heard tell about things like this, but never seen 'em with my own eyes. Never found any the family, y'know. None of them. Guess you must've went to school with Freddy Junior, same as my boy, Barry, didn't you—"

Les suddenly discovered he was talking to himself. He looked left, right, and all around. There was no sheet-covered boy anywhere.

A cold sweat broke out across his forehead, mixing with the bitter rain.

IDA VOWELS' hoarse, age-dimmed screams blended in an eerie symphony with her honking geese. She scurried from the clothesline, slopping through the backyard sludge. The frenzied birds flapped away toward a neighbor's pond, terrified. Her hounds were gone, having fled at the first sight of the thing that came crawling out of the cornfield.

The biggest shock was that Ida had recognized it.

She'd seen the thing every day for years among her neighbor's crops, a twelve foot titan of tobacco sticks and rags guarding over the sprouting stalks. It had vanished since that infamous April 3rd cyclone, gone and forgotten. Until now.

The scarecrow slithered toward her on its bloated hay-filled belly, weighted down from the driving rain. There was no face to speak of, merely worm-holes and wrinkles twisted into burlap. As the thing crept toward her, the soggy stuffed limbs flopped hideously, bleeding a trail of straw which writhed and squirmed in the puddles like anemic worms.

Ida's narrow back pressed against the woodshed, the rain clattering on its tin roof in a deafening torrent. Slumping to her boney knees, she gasped with asthma, too weak to rise.

No doubt about it, she realized, trembling. It was the End of the World.

Then, another tempest struck.

It was a living storm, shaped like a giant bundle of bones, as far as Ida could tell through the downpour. It leaped upon the thing from the cornfield, within mere yards of reaching her, clashing and thrashing in a savage fury. Sledge-hard fists struck, and uncoiling limbs of rags and straw flailed, fighting back like a great octopus.

Everything was happening too fast, too terrible.

The little duck pond erupted as the wrestling apparitions struck the surface like cannon fire, sinking out of sight. Ida's fogged bifocals were useless in the blinding, deafening rain. Her breath strained and twisted in her throat, seized with a full attack. She was blacking out.

Then, through the misty wreath of her dimming vision, Ida beheld a single figure emerging from the pond. It was like a man, but larger than anyone she had ever seen. His skeleton seemed to show through his skin, glowing white like the lines on the highway at night. Or, perhaps, it was some kind of Halloween suit with painted bones.

The giant came nearer, reaching out to her. Mercifully, in a swirl of vertigo, Ida collapsed.

IDA'S LITTLE house felt chilled and cramped to the giant, his head nearly scraping the ceiling as he carried her like a ragdoll to the living room couch. He tossed more kindling in the woodstove and swiftly searched for her telephone, finding it fixed to the kitchen wall by the well-stocked cupboards. It was an old fashioned instrument, the type with a separate ear and mouth piece. Been a long time since he'd seen one like it.

He made a quick study of Ida's mail to obtain her identity, then cranked the phone into life.

"Ambulance needed at Ida Vowels' farm," the skull-mask only slightly muffled his deep baritone. "Respiratory seizure, probably asthmatic. Emergency."

And he ended the connection.

The giant remained with Ida as she fitfully slept, until the approaching sirens signaled his rapid exit out into the masking rain.

CHAPTER FOUR
"Autumn in the Spider-Pit"

"THEY WON'T be over-cooked, will they? Last time it was like gnawing on charcoal. I refuse to pay for that. A moron can fry a hamburger. It's not rocket science. If you get it right one time, it should always be right. There's no excuse. Okay, guess I'll try the deluxe platter again. Better not be over-cooked."

"Want fries or onion rings with that, ma'am?" Molly literally bit her tongue, forcing herself to be polite.

Rodney Ottersback, the district manager, was there, keeping a piercing hawk's eye on everyone. He had two eyes, actually, but there was a twisted way he'd raise one arrogant eyebrow that tended to obscure the other orb. Ottersback always singled out Molly during these unexpected visits, particularly picking on her apparent lack of enthusiasm toward difficult patrons. The district manager was proud of the anxiety he inspired in his underlings, and he was a company man through and through.

Molly made a point of counting back the complaining customer's change much more kindly than usual. Still, she felt Ottersback's cyclopsian stare burning a hole in the back of her neck. With a slightly stifled sigh, she turned to face the music.

"Watch that smirk, Aldrich," Ottersback gritted, sweating through his dress shirt. "You'd better pay attention to your business. Employee reviews are coming up in just a few weeks, and you might just find yourself holding an empty sack."

Whatever the heck that meant.

Molly bit her tongue, again. It was getting pretty sore.

"Sorry, Mr. Ottersback. I wasn't smirking. Must have something in my eye. Probably an eyelash."

Ottersback glowered.

"Well, don't stand there blinking like you're afflicted! We can't have the counter littered with germ-ridden stray eye lashes. That's so unsanitary it's not even funny. Go to the restroom and take care of it."

She nodded, forcing an appreciative smile.

It was a quiet night, but then Tuesdays usually were. The parking lot was empty and there hadn't been more than a half dozen jiggles at the door all evening. Their pronounced lack of motivation made the district manager's unannounced arrival all the more merciless.

Finally, Ottersback had parked himself on the phone, apparently jabbering to a girlfriend, while Lea and Cindy pretended extra attentiveness to the gurgling grease baskets. Both kept quiet till Molly sought sanctuary within the lavatory.

"Bad enough that Otters-quack is here, but we gotta work with the weirdo, too," Cindy said, overly salting the blistering fries. "What's she doing out on a school night, anyways?"

Lea kept an eye on the restroom door.

"She graduated or dropped-out. I dunno. My brother Bobby told me. Guess she'll be here a lot more now."

"That stinks. Chick gives me the creeps. I heard she burned down her house, or something," Cindy didn't notice the onion rings had sputtered from golden brown to deep mahogany.

"I heard that, too," Lea nodded, eyes growing round. "Mom said she'd gone from one foster home after another, until the Hutchins finally took her in last year."

"She reads all them witchy books, too."

"And doesn't date."

"At all?"

"Nope. Bobby dared Jimmy Brunner to ask her out once."

"And?"

"Said she'd 'rather not'."

"Seriously? She said that? To Jimmy Brunner? Meow."

"Shhh…" Lea hissed, as Molly made her way back behind the counter.

Molly frowned faintly, bowing her head at Ottersback's grimace from the wall phone. She knew the girls had been talking about her, too, but that was nothing new. There had to be a better job somewhere.

Suddenly, from Cindy's neglect, the grease basket over-heated, bursting into flames. A vicious plume lashed out, igniting Lea's sleeve. Ottersback cursed loudly and stumbled forward, entangled in the phone cord. Cindy and Lea screamed in panicked pandemonium .

Later, neither the girls, nor certainly Ottersback, would agree on what had happened next. It would remain a somewhat sinister mystery, re-told around the sizzling grease baskets from then on.

Molly gasped, rushing toward the fire extinguisher, her slender hand outstretched. The blaze from Lea's sleeve seemed to dance through the air, drawn to Molly like a magnet, coiling around her wrist. Then, the flames promptly vanished.

It looked as though the fire was absorbed into Molly herself, but that was crazy, and no one ever described it that way in later gossip. Not even Lea. But she knew that was exactly what had happened.

Lea was unhurt, suffering merely a scorched sleeve. Cindy immediately ran toward the restroom, hiding herself in the stall. Ottersback gaped and gawked, and that caterpillar eyebrow slowly crawled to meet his oily hairline.

"You're fired, Aldrich!" his puffed face purpled. "No excuse for such carelessness! Get your things and vacate the premises at once! Immediately, I said!"

Lea watched through the window as Molly walked away down the lonely avenue, not completely comprehending why she suddenly felt like crying.

CRISP AUTUMN leaves scuttled and scurried at Molly's feet, appearing to follow her in the gusting wind. Even under the muted streetlights the swirling patches of orange, gold, and crimson reminded her of fluttering flames. The girl shivered, and her stomach bothered her a bit. That was so weird about the fire… but she had seen weirder things, too. Stubbornly, she shook her dark tousled hair. Best not to think about that.

Molly had already ditched her teal-colored work smock in a vacant trashcan, which was exactly where it belonged. No way did she want to drag its bad karma back into her damp little basement apartment. That place was crappy enough already.

Fumbling for her keys, oppressively lost in thought, Molly very nearly stumbled upon the black cat.

"Oh," she jumped a little, startled. "Where did you come from?"

The animal just sat there on the concrete steps, unblinking. The girl extended her hand, then thought the better of it as the cat's hackles prickled like porcupine quills.

"Be that way, then," she grumbled, squeezing aside into the door.

Molly descended the stairs without flipping on the light, feeling more comforted by the dark. What a miserable night. She just wanted to go and hide.

After securely locking her door, she tossed her keys on the fake marble countertop, and plopped down in the patched recliner that doubled as her bed. No use turning on any lamps and adding to the electric bill. The lights would only make her think of the fire, anyway, which she fearfully wanted to forget.

So, Molly just sat there, in the dark, deciding whether or not she wanted to bawl.

HUH? WHAT time was it?

Molly twitched suddenly, surprised that she had dozed for a while. The luminous green hands on the wall clock glowed half past midnight. She wiped her moist cheeks with a sleeve and decided she needed company, on the double.

Despite herself, Molly smiled slightly in the gloom, remembering there was an old Mummy movie on the midnight late show. Her mood brightened a bit as she leaned over, switching on her junky little black and white TV.

At once, she literally screamed.

The black cat, in total obsidian majesty, was leering at Molly from the top of the flickering set.

"What th—? But—? H-how did you—?" she stammered.

Molly glanced quickly at the door, finding the chain still fastened.

"You... you must've sneaked in while I went down the stairs in the dark," the girl stood unnerved, uncertain what to do next.

The animal glowered, unmoving.

"Sure are pretty, aren't you?" Molly softened her voice. "Too bad I'm allergic to cats. Guess it doesn't matter, though. I'm not allowed to have pets in this place. Still, I figure it'll be all right for you to visit just a little while."

She rummaged through her tiny icebox.

"Lemme see... okay, you're in luck. I still have some milk and a bit of tuna salad leftover. C'mon, you're welcome to share it."

After a long suspicious pause, the cat began lapping delicately at the saucer of milk. Molly didn't feel very hungry, but was glad to have a guest. The feline sipped her fill, and sat again, slightly shivering from the ice-cold milk.

"Yeah, sorry it's so chilly down here," dragged out an old sweatshirt, making it into a pallet next to her chair. "They haven't turned the heat on yet. I've been sleeping in my winter parka and three pairs of socks. This should be comfy enough for you, better than outside in the alley, anyway. Hop on down and give it a try."

But the cat just sat and stared.

"Ooookay. Guess it's warmer up there on the TV, anyway. Sorry, I'm just a stupid girl. And you're... well, a cat. You know best."

Funny, Molly had just noticed that her nose wasn't tickling. No itchy eyes either. Usually she'd be sneezing her brains out by now. Regardless of the aloof 'Here's looking down at you' attitude, she was starting to sort of like this mysterious feline.

"So, what do you think of my humble abode?" the girl's arm theatrically swept the dank little room. "I call it 'The Spider Pit.' You'll see why if you examine the cluttered webs in the four corners of the ceiling."

The black cat glanced up, unimpressed.

"Y'know," Molly fretted, "I really like this place, spiders and all. It's my first real home. Wish I could stay, but I... I got fired tonight. Sure don't want to go back to the Hutchins'. And I know they wouldn't let me keep you."

The cat yawned. Molly giggled. It felt good to laugh.

"Really keeping you riveted with interest, eh? Alright, smarty pants, why not tell me who's hiring right now? Preferably somewhere outside the gourmet greasy-spoon dining industry. Any clues?"

Molly's softly curved jaw dropped in astonishment, as the cat's paw purposely seemed to turn up the TV's volume.

"It's scary! It's screamy! It's screwy!" a weird voice cackled, as cartoon Jack O'Lanterns and animated skeletons danced across the screen. *"Shake with laughs! Shiver with suspense! Tremble with thrills!"*

The girl knelt down in front of the set, mesmerized.

"See live monsters! See real ghosts! Guys—bring your girlfriends! Girls—see if your boyfriends are men... or mice! An eerily equal opportunity employer! Opening Halloween night, and one night only, at the Creepy, Crawley, Carnival of Chaos! Admission is free to anyone with a heartbeat! Free! Free! Free! At the Woodland Fairgrounds this Halloween Night! Keep watching the skies!"

The cat jumped down from the television and noisily scratched at the door. Molly unlocked it and curiously followed the animal up the stairs. Once outside, it sat on its haunches and peered intensely up at the rolling clouds. Molly couldn't help but follow the cat's gaze.

Soaring, beaming, grinning high in the night sky was a swarm of pumpkin-shaped searchlights, triangular eyes and jagged mouths soundlessly laughing across the heavens. Molly detected that their orange origins shone from the east, from the direction of the Woodland Fairgrounds.

"That's a long ways off," she murmured, more to herself than the cat. "At least thirty miles. Well, I don't have anything else to do. Maybe they'd give me a job. C'mon, cat... let's get going."

The girl and cat began their long late night hike, and both kept watching the skies.

"The All-Grey Lady"

DARLENE WHELAN had never heard anything like it. Not even eight a.m. yet and the phone at the sheriff's office was ringing off the hook.

"Say again, Mrs. Strieble? Ooookay... hmm. Yes ma'am, of course, I've heard of chickens running around with their heads cut off—but not butchered pigs. Jumped down from your smokehouse wall, did they? Try not to take so many of those back-ache pills of yours. I'm hanging up now, Mrs. Strieble."

A whole world of trouble was erupting all over the county, far from the usual sorts of problems. And the day was still early.

"Hello, Sheriff's Office," Darlene answered the nineteenth call of the morning. "Mr. Corbett? Waitaminute. Slow down, I don't understand. Say again? There's something howling in your chimney? Sure it's not the wind? No, I don't mean your stomach troubles. Y'know, sometimes squirrels will—well, yes, squirrels chatter and don't howl, but... all right, Mr. Corbett. I'll tell the sheriff when he comes in."

At first Darlene's pretty eyes had scoffed, annoyed at the presumed prank calls, but then folks she knew well and trusted—including members of her church—also frantically phoned, complaining of the strangest things.

"Sheriff's Office, how may I help you—oh. Father Clancy, thank heaven. You wouldn't believe the clamor of calls I've been get—what's that? Oh. Oh my goodness. Well, I mean, uh, are you sure? You actually heard the gravestones in the cemetery, uh… whispering? Well, what about Father Luckett, did you tell h—oh. Oh, I see. He heard them last evening, too? I… I don't know what to say. Oh dear. Well, I'm not sure if you should tell the Archbishop, but I will certainly let the sheriff know."

When Darlene's sister called, she was starting to take the strangeness all very seriously.

"Just try to keep calm, Kay. Why don't you and Pete wait in the pick-up for Uncle Les? That's right, he should be here any minute and I'm sure he'll come over right away. If it happens again, just drive and get out of there. Y'hear?"

Darlene glanced at the wall clock and fretted. Two minutes past eight. Where in the world was the sheriff? He was hardly ever late, and never on a Monday. Why hadn't he called in?

"Good morning, dearie. I've come to see the sheriff."

A tall old lady stood in the open doorway, partially eclipsed by the glaring sun behind her. Darlene squinted, shading a hand over her delicate brow. There was something mirage-like about the moment, almost like a dream. *Great gobs of gravy*, she shuddered. How much more weirdness could she take this morning?

"Oh my gracious," the old woman clucked. "You look like you've seen a ghost. I'm right sorry. Didn't mean to spook you none."

She was quietly, but impeccably dressed, in a neat jacket and skirt of grey tweed, with old fashioned button-up boots, and moved toward Darlene's desk in a sort of softly clacking, gliding motion. Her silver-grey hair was twisted tightly in a perfect bun, without a single strand out of place. Almost everything about her seemed very old, but also fresh and full of energy.

"My uncle, umm, that is, the sheriff isn't here," Darlene slightly stammered. "I'm afraid you'll—"

"No need to be afraid, dearie. Not so long as the sun is shining and we all can see what is what," the old woman's eyes shone with a gentle humor, but her fixed gleaming grin wasn't quite right.

She gripped a few stapled papers in her immaculate pearl grey gloves. Her dark eyes softened, but the shrewd lipless smile broadened weirdly. At a closer inspection, Darlene noticed that the woman's face had been thickly smeared with pancake make-up and not too good a job either. Her face was a bit too pink to look real, the single flaw in her neat and presentable appearance. She sure was an odd old bird.

"Would you be a dear and give these to the sheriff?"

"Give me what?" Sheriff Les Charles came stomping in, already not in the best of moods.

The old woman gracefully spun toward him as if she was standing on a spindle.

"It's my carnival license for your fairgrounds, Sheriff. All signed sealed and nicely legal."

The sheriff stared warily at the documents, taking them with an obvious reluctance.

"Oh. Well, that's fine, Mrs. Uhh—"

"Miss Grimalkin, Sheriff. Must say I'm surprised. Last time you told me you'd never forget a name as odd as mine," she snickered, wagging a long grey-gloved finger at him.

Les blushed a bit. He felt stifled and somewhat cornered. He wanted the weird old woman out of his office.

"Sorry, Mrs.—ah, I mean Miss Grimalkin. How long will you and your carnival be stayin'?"

She exhaled a not unmusical giggle.

"Mercy me, but you're absent-minded today! Just until after Halloween, silly. The permit is paid up for that long. Now I know you've got your hands full, so I'll wish you and this pretty young lady a very lovely morning."

Les and Darlene watched as Miss Grimalkin glided from their office out into the blinding morning sun.

"Crazy ol' coot," he muttered. "Should have my head examined for letting that freak sideshow of hers park at our fairgrounds. Ugh... You wouldn't believe the mornin' I've had already. Everyone complainin' of the strangest things. If this was April 1st, I'd understand it."

"Not been a picnic here either," Darlene jabbed a fistful of messages in his face.

Les thumbed through Darlene's scribbles, shaking his head all the while.

"Okay, lemme see," he said. "Melvin Dowell's well water has changed to blood? Probably just red clay that got into the cistern somehow. Uh-oh... Barbara Myers claims she saw the Goat-Boy again? That's the third time since last summer. It'll be Bigfoot next. Okay, lemme see about the rest of these messages—"

Darlene stopped him, fearful tears brimming in her eyes.

"Uncle Les, please!" Darlene sobbed. "Kay and Pete... they're in trouble!"

"Cripesakes," Les grumbled, "your sister and brother, too? Was there a full moon last night or somethin'? Everybody's goin' nuts. What're they seein'? Spooks? Flying saucers? What?"

The girl took a deep, shuddering breath.

"It... it's their barn."

"Well? What about it?"

"It's... crawling."

The Sheriff frowned.

"Kay's barn is crawlin'? Crawlin' with what? Mice? Rats? What?"

"No… no, you don't understand," Darlene's voice cracked to a whisper. "Kay says the barn is crawling. By itself. It's creeping closer and closer to her house…!"

"MORE PANCAKES, hon? Looks to me like you could use 'em."

Molly nodded shyly, staring wondrously at the hot buttery stacks. Even after already devouring her first plateful, they still smelled heavenly. She hadn't eaten this well in quite a while.

Glancing out the large front window of *Aunt Ethel's Melon Patch Diner*, Molly made certain the black cat was still sitting outside on the sidewalk. The animal was there, all right. The cat stared back at the girl with an air of utter impatience.

"Some more orange juice, too?"

"Yes, please. Thank you, ma'am," Molly mustered a meek smile.

"Oh, landsakes," the middle-aged woman in the crisp aqua uniform laughed. "Call me 'Aunt Ethel', darlin'. Around these parts, everybody does. Say, that your cat?"

Molly wasn't exactly sure how to answer.

"Um, well, I guess so. I mean, we just sort of recently ran into each other."

Aunt Ethel wiped down another table while admiring the glossy black feline.

"Used to have a cat like that when I was a girl," she mused. "Called him Trey 'cause he'd lost a hind leg in a trap. Don't let that worry you none, though, 'cause he could still chase away them dern rabbits from our garden like nobody's business. Wonder if your cat would like some sausage? I always cook too much. I'll wrap some up and you can take it with you."

Aunt Ethel disappeared in the kitchen for a moment, and then returned with the little package of cooked meat.

"Here you are, hon. By the way, if I'm not bein' too nosey, where're you goin'? Visitin' family or somethin'?"

Molly swallowed her last scrumptious forkful of syrup-smothered pancake.

"Looking for a new job, I suppose," Molly slid up from the red vinyl booth, putting on her jacket. "Saw an ad on TV last night for some kind of carnival or something. Spent the night following those Jack O' Lantern searchlights , but I got lost when the sun came up."

"Lawsy me, child!" Aunt Ethel exclaimed. "You mean you've been walkin' all night? Where'd you start off from?"

The girl was suddenly embarrassed, feeling more than a little bit foolish.

"From Valley Station," she admitted. "It *has* been a pretty long hike. You see, I lost my job yesterday and I guess I wasn't thinking too straight."

Aunt Ethel patted Molly softly on the sleeve.

"Now don't you fret. I need a waitress here, if you'd like the job. Bet you'd get along fine with my daughter Charlotte. She works here, too, after school and on weekends, and she's about your age. What'd ya think?"

Molly wasn't sure.

"Well, I mean, I'm sort of on my own. I still need to move out of my old place, and… "

The woman casually waved a hand and chuckled.

"Shucks, my oldest boy is away in the service. You could have his room for a while, if you want it. Bring your cat, too. Why, I could drive you to Valley Station and help you get your stuff this evenin'."

This was all a bit too much and a bit too fast. Molly stood there blinking and tongue-tied.

"Why," Molly finally asked, "are you being so nice to me?"

Aunt Ethel smiled softly, and a bit sadly.

"Well, you seem to have some trouble, I reckon that you don't want to bother me with. That's okay, I won't be nosey. Let's just say you remind me of someone I used to know, a long time ago. Tell you what… think it over and let me know later today. That okay?"

Molly's head was practically spinning.

"Thanks. I will. Um, how much do I owe you for the pancakes and juice?"

"Tell you what…" Aunt Ethel rubbed her chin, "I'll make you a deal. See that box of fruit jars? Take 'em downstairs for me and we'll call it even. I'd rather not go down that spooky basement, if I can help it. If you're going to work here, you might as well learn where everything is kept."

Sounded like a bargain to Molly, since she had only a few dollars. She packed up the boxes and carefully navigated her way down the wooden stairs into the gloomy grey basement. There might have been a light switch, but the girl couldn't find it. The space below was sparingly illuminated from a single sunbeam projected through a small dusty window.

No doubt about it, she couldn't blame Aunt Ethel one bit. This was a very creepy place.

It was also quite cold, there in the basement. Unnaturally so. As Molly first set foot on the dank concrete floor she could immediately see the frosty puffs of her own breath. Suddenly, she heard a slight swishing sound from behind a row of stacked shelves. Fearful of rats, she spun and started to flee up the steps.

"Can… can you find my momma?" a small, timid voice stammered from the murk.

Molly squinted her eyes, and then sighed with relief. It was only a kid. A boy about nine or ten years old, from his size and sound, oddly draped in a plain white bed sheet, and standing alone in a dark corner.

"Oh hey," she scrunched down a bit, smiling. "You scared me. What are you doing down here all by yourself?"

The shroud stood still as a statue for a long moment. Molly could barely make out a pair of bashful blue eyes staring from the uneven holes cut from the sheet.

"I'm hiding from a monster," he replied, no stutter that time.

"Well, I'm sure your disguise will scare it away. I'm Molly. What's your name?"

Another long, awkward pause.

"Freddy Fridley. Have you seen my momma? Looked all over. Can't find her nowhere."

Something wasn't quite right about this. Molly straightened slowly to her full height and turned toward the steps, glancing back at Freddy from over her shoulder.

"C'mon upstairs with me and I'll find her for you," she suggested, the fine hairs on the nape of her neck were starting to prickle.

Freddy hesitated, then reluctantly rustled forward. Molly's brown eyes grew round. Her jaw dropped. The boy covered with the sheet had stepped into the sunbeam and had virtually vanished. Only a whisper of a hint remained of him, like a drape of cellophane immersed in a spotlight.

Molly lost no time scampering up the warped wooden stairs of the haunted basement without looking back.

Her heart pounding, she had just seen her first honest-to-goodness ghost, and that was one ghost too many.

"The Crawling Barn"

I T WAS unreal, but there was no denying it.

Sheriff Les Charles could hardly believe his own eyes, but there in the bright and shimmering afternoon sunshine Kay Whelan's weathered old barn was slowly crawling, actually moving on its own, ever closer to her farmhouse.

It was eerie and unearthly. The dry grey boards and rusty tin roof creaked and screeched with each writhing, predatory, inexplicable motion.

"How can that be happenin', Uncle Les?" Pete breathed, wringing his nervous hands on the front of his faded bib overalls.

Les chuckled not too convincingly, turning toward his nephew and niece's pleading doe-like eyes, so much like their sister Darlene's. He was more than their mother's brother, he was their godfather and had known them since they were born. Clearly Kay and Pete were terrified, and Les was trying best he could to set them at ease.

"Sure wish I could say, Pete," Les laughed a little. "In my old drinkin' days I could explain it."

Kay curled an arm around her brother's elbow, attempting to comfort him.

"Maybe…" she suggested, "it's from all that rain we had last week? You know, like maybe it's a mud-slide?"

The sheriff shook his head.

"That'd be a right good idea if the barn wasn't creepin' uphill. Gotta admit, that's one of the most dat-blasted things I ever saw. Either of you look inside yet?"

"Y-you kiddin'?" Pete's voice quivered.

"I reckon that would've been kinda foolish at that," Les patted Pete's shoulder. "Did you notice anything odd about the barn in the past few days? Strange noises? Odd smells? Anything out of the ordinary?"

"Well," Kay remembered, "our chickens have kept away from it since Sunday."

"And we couldn't get the horses to go inside last night, so they stayed in the pasture," Pete added.

"Yeah, that's right," his sister confirmed. "There was a slinky black cat around here for the past couple weeks, too, thinning out the mice, I guess. Haven't seen it lately."

The sheriff had heard enough, and knew what he had to do next.

"Awright," he tried to hide a shiver and drew his gun. "Y'all keep back. I'm gonna go take a closer look."

Miraculously, the old barn had continued to crawl the entire time they'd been talking. It moved with lurching persistence, like the minute hand of a colossal clicking clock. Les forced himself forward, finding some confidence in the iron weight of his heavy revolver. He reached for the weathered barn door and wrenched it open, took a deep breath, and went inside.

Abruptly, the structure halted in its uncanny motion.

Gaping grey gloom met the sheriff's eyes, with pale hay-baled monoliths stacked almost to the lofty ceiling. He took a cautious step. And another. The soles of his boots scraped softly on the damp dirt floor.

Then something… squished.

The sheriff winced as his nostrils stung with a sulfurous stench. The flashlight sputtered and sparked, finally blazing brightly and slicing through the murk. His eyes focused on the floor as he gaped, frozen with fear.

A multitude of quivering grapefruit-sized bubbles swamped the bottom of the barn. A closer study revealed long, clacking, needle-like legs, like those of a spindly spider, attached to the amber vein-lined living globules. They swarmed across the straw and the dirt, grotesquely perching on the lawn-mower and plow. And they didn't end there.

Sweeping his flashlight back up and around, Les was sickened to see the crawling globs had also conquered the walls and the ceiling beams of the old barn. They were everywhere. Impossible to count.

Bracing himself, with jaw muscles clenched, the sheriff beamed the light directly at a single crawling creature clinging to a gnarled old post. Repulsed, he shrank back slightly stumbling.

A mass of tiny, spidery horrors cluttered alive inside the monster's bulbous semi-transparent body. Awful. Terrifying.

Les felt a sudden thorny prickling under his collar.

And the crawling blobs sprang at him.

"DON'T LOOK at me that way," Molly grumbled to the black cat. "I wasn't being rude to that nice lady. I never really believed in ghosts before, but I know what I saw. No one can blame me for not wanting to work at a place with a haunted basement."

The cat kept easy pace with the girl, trotting down the lonely gravel road.

"Besides, she gave us directions to the Fairgrounds, didn't she? So, it wasn't like she was mad at me or anything."

The black cat glanced up with an air of indifference.

"Yeah, well," Molly slowly shook her head, "I guess I did run out of there kind of fast. She gave us a free breakfast, too. Okay, great. Now I officially feel like a scaredy-brat."

Molly glanced over her shoulder and considered returning to the diner to say she was sorry, but she had walked so far already. Surely she and the cat would come upon the Fairgrounds at any moment. It would be silly to turn back now.

The old country road began to widen a bit, giving Molly hope that she'd soon reach her destination. It was impossible to tell exactly where she and the cat were, most of the time. A neglected cornfield with a battalion of ancient scarecrows loomed to the left of the road, while a ponderous patch of yellow pumpkins ripened in the afternoon sunshine on the right.

The girl grinned at the squint in the cat's fussy green eyes.

"All right, you win," she even giggled a little at the feline's dramatic glare. "After we see, um, whoever about the job in the carnival, we'll retrace our steps to apologize. Say, I wonder if—"

A single, blood-curdling scream stopped Molly and the cat in their tracks. The girl paused, tingling with goose-bumps. Suddenly, another yell—louder and more frantic than before. Sounded like a man, she thought. What kind of thing could make a grown man scream like that?

Molly wanted to run... but in which direction?

The black cat decided for her, racing away around a willow-edged bend in the road, directly toward the terrible cries.

There was no choice for Molly, except to follow.

"**W**ell, whatever they are... looks like the sunshine is dryin' 'em up, like salt on a slug," Pete anxiously observed.

He and Kay stared at the squirming multi-legged blobs as they crumbled to a soft orange ash under the bright sun. Les was still wildly wringing out his jacket, hunting for more of the little crawling creatures. He was lucky. No more in sight.

"It's the sun that's killing them all right," Kay gripped her brother's elbow, stepping further back. "What kind of crazy bugs are they? I've never seen anything like them."

"Neither has anyone else, I reckon," Les scratched his head, trying to think. "What I *do* know is that there are about a million of those ugly little things crawlin' and squirmin' inside your barn—so many of 'em that they're causin' the whole blamed structure to shift and slide off its foundation!"

There was a long pause, as the unreality of the moment took root.

"I—I wonder if they're poisonous? They look poisonous to me," Kay shuddered.

"Wouldn't be at all surprised," Les nodded. "At least the daylight is keepin' them from escapin' outside."

"But what happens after the sun goes down?" Pete hoarsely whispered.

The sheriff and his niece and nephew traded darting, troubled glances. What would happen, indeed?

"Look, this is gonna be a tough decision... I know your daddy built this barn with his own hands," Les said slowly, "but if we were to set a fire—"

"Burn the barn," Kay understood instantly. "Let's do it. It's the only way to be sure."

They looked at Pete.

"Without the barn the bugs can't hide from the sun. Yup, we gotta burn it, right down to the ground," he agreed.

Sheriff Les took a long, deep breath of regret.

"Awright, but we gotta do it real quick—before the barn gets any closer to your house," he hurried toward the patrol car. "I have a can of gasoline and some road flares in the trunk, and I'll radio Brandenburg for the fire department. We're gonna need them out here."

Les anxiously fumbled with his keys, dropping them twice before managing to unlock the trunk. Once inside he rummaged hastily through its cluttered contents. Immediately his heart sank.

"Dag-nab-bit! I plum forgot that I used the gas to fill up Carl Brown's stalled pick-up last evenin'. No flares either. Barry's been playin' around in here again. Gotta talk to that boy. Awright, now what're we gonna—huh—?"

A sleek black cat suddenly sped past Les, followed by a petite dark-haired girl racing after the animal. Both seemed to come out of nowhere. And they were headed directly toward the crawling barn.

"Hey, you—! Girl! Whaddaya think you're doin'?! Keep away from there!" the sheriff shouted.

Too late. Both the cat and the girl had already vanished inside.

Molly skidded to an abrupt halt. The cat had seemed to melt within the darkness of the barn. The air itself didn't smell right. Somewhere in the murk the black cat hissed. The girl could also hear the straw rustling on the floor, and rapid clacking sounds resounding from the boards and beams surrounding her. It was as if the shadows themselves were alive.

Then, she saw them. Dimly. Horribly. Like the first flickering of an on-coming nightmare.

They flooded ominously, hungrily toward Molly. Almost immediately the creatures had surrounded her, multi-legged monstrosities with bloated bodies the size of softballs. Glittering, unblinking, pin-prick eyes chilled her blood.

Molly outstretched her hands, shielding her face, as the awful spider-things prepared to leap.

They never had the chance.

It started as a mere tingling in her finger-tips, sort of like the sensation when your hands are asleep. Then, Molly felt a hint of the heat-blast upon her face.

Incredibly, spectacularly, tongues of blue and orange flame surged from the girl's fingers. The fiery streams writhed through the dank atmosphere, seeming almost alive. The crawling, clattering things were briefly illuminated in their full horror—then instantaneously obliterated into puffs of steaming dust.

Molly's fire poured across the dirt floor like magma, coiling up support beams, and sizzling toward the ceiling. The weathered wood and bales of dried straw caught quickly. The barn was an instant inferno.

The girl stood there, mesmerized among the raging blaze. She still felt no great heat. Had no trouble breathing. It didn't make sense.

Molly and the flames were one.

Sheriff Les burst into the burning barn just in time to see Molly escape through the back wall, the charred timbers seeming to melt away like tissue paper as the girl passed through. It was the choking, blinding smoke causing the mirage, he reasoned, and fought his way back out into the cool open air.

"Did… did you see… did the girl get out?" Les asked, struggling with his breath.

Pete pointed at the deep tree-line in the field beyond the raging barn.

"She ran off into the woods, chasing after that black cat!"

"They didn't look like they were hurt—just scared! Where did they come from anyway?" Kay wondered.

Les was bent over coughing, leaning over with his hands on his knees.

"Get on the radio to your sister," he ordered, shaking his head. "Tell her to send the fire department—all three engines. And when they ask, and they will, neither of you know how the barn caught fire. Get me?"

They nodded and ran toward the patrol car.

The sheriff stood and watched the blazing building for a moment longer. It was awful to behold. Already the ceiling beams were snapping and the great roof collapsed upon itself. Nothing could escape.

Satisfied, Les turned toward the dark woods. Who was that teenager? How did the fire start? What kind of craziness was going on in his normally quiet and peaceful, even boring community? Was it the End of the World? He had to find that girl. Maybe she had some answers.

The thick canopy of the forest turned the bright afternoon to twilight with his first step. No sign of the girl. And what was the deal with that cat?

A slight and sudden rustling behind the sheriff snapped his musing.

He whirled around expecting to see the petite teenager, but instead found a veritable seven and a half foot giant dressed in a macabre Halloween skeleton costume.

Les backed up, fumbling for his pistol.

"Put away your weapon, Sheriff," baleful yellow eyes burned from the sockets of the skull mask. "It's time you and I had a talk."

"Return of the Goat-Boy"

MOLLY RAN blindly through the shadowed woods. Low whip-like limbs lashed her cheeks, and thorny weeds gouged at her ankles. She didn't dare to glance over her shoulder even once. The spider-things might be chasing her.

Unexpectedly, Molly emerged from dark green gloom into the blinding yellow haze of a claustrophobic cornfield. Her head swirled and she pitched hard to the ground, the wind rustling through the surrounding crackling stalks. She felt sick, haunted by the fire in the barn and how it had happened.

"Did I really do *that*...?" she knelt trembling on the moist earth, staring at her smooth open palms.

Molly's deep red nail polish had melted into her cuticles like blood, and the cuffs of her jacket were slightly singed. She smelled of burning wood and smoky straw. Funny how she suddenly felt feverish and then very cold, shivering in the bright afternoon sunshine.

The black cat emerged from among the cornstalks and sat down, gazing at the girl with a cool yellow-green glare. Molly wanted to cry, but the tears wouldn't come. Somewhere in the distance the wail of the fire trucks' sirens eerily harmonized.

"Well, my-oh-my! Autumn is here, earlier than I expected!" came a musical giggle from behind.

Molly sprang to her feet, startled by a tall grey old lady. The black cat immediately leaped into the woman's arms and began purring loudly.

"Don't look at me like that, child," the old woman grinned. "I know we've been in the fall season for weeks, I'm not that crazy. I meant 'Autumn' the cat. Looks like you've taken good care of her. Very good, indeed. Very much appreciated."

Molly blinked.

"Uh, you're welcome, I guess. Your cat's name is Autumn?"

"My cat?" the grey lady's laugh turned a bit too shrill. "Well, cats don't really belong to anyone. They choose who they want to be with or not to be with. Cats never really lose the wild jungle sap in their blood, you know. There's a saber-tooth lurking beneath every sleek and pampered coat. Oh, and I wasn't thanking you, child. I was thanking Autumn. Yes, that's one of her names, among many more."

The girl blinked again, shaking her head.

"I don't understand, ma'am. This cat followed me all the way from Valley Station. How could her home be out here—over thirty miles away? And how did you find us in a cornfield in the middle of nowhere?"

"My, my, my!" she clapped her grey-gloved hands together. "One question at a time, dearie. Cats know best. You need to understand that right off the bat. Ah! Cat! Bat! What a lovely pun! Well, I'm parched. Come along, Miss Molly. Let's have some tea."

The grey lady turned, motioning for the girl to follow, but Molly stopped cold in her tracks.

"H-how… how do you know my name?" she stammered in shock.

"Try using your noggin, child," the grey lady grinned. "How do you think I know?"

Molly turned even paler. She suddenly wanted to run, but didn't know where.

"You... umm... read my mind...?"

The old woman's laughter rang up and down the musical scale. "Oh my, no. No, indeed," she winked at Molly, knowingly. "You wouldn't really want me to do that, would you?"

No doubt about it, the girl decided. The weird grey lady was nutty as a filbert.

"Then... how?" Molly wondered, abruptly more curious than creeped.

Autumn the black cat stared at the girl from over the old woman's shoulder.

"How do I know anything?" the old woman explained, "Why, Autumn told me. She whispered it, of course, but she can be quite chatty when the fancy is upon her. Just you wait."

Yup, Molly had the grey lady properly pegged. Categorically coo-coo.

"You may call me Miss Grimalkin," she curtsied to Molly with genuine grace. "Very pleased to finally meet you, by the way. I would tell you my first name, but it's quite unpronounceable. Oh, and we're not really 'in the middle of nowhere', as you so quaintly put it. See for yourself!"

Within just a few steps, Molly found herself out of the cornfield's clutter and into the cool open air of the Fairgrounds. High-peaked orange and black tents were pitched, while luridly painted show-fronts and stomach-wrenching thrill rides were being clanked and clattered into assembly. Although Molly couldn't see the carnival workers very clearly at that distance, somehow they didn't move right, their elbows and knees seemingly bending at the wrong places.

Grey old Miss Grimalkin politely raised the door-flap of her tent, and Molly walked with her into another world.

"**H**OW DO I know I can trust you?" Sheriff Les warily holstered his weapon.

The costumed giant stood among the canopy of maple and oak, a towering figure of stillness.

"I did save your life," the jaw of the skull mask moved, as if alive.

The sheriff nodded, and slowly let out a shuddering breath.

"Sure enough," he propped up a boot upon a fallen log. "You wanted to talk. Well, let's have it."

The heavy skull head tilted slightly.

"Your community is in deadly danger. Worse than you already know. We're here to help, but your assistance will be necessary," the Skeleton's voice was low and deep, like thunder under control.

"Who's 'we'?" Les squinted, still skeptical.

The sheriff flinched a bit backwards as the Skeleton took a single step closer. He really was massive.

"That needs to remain a mystery," the giant replied in hollow baritone.

"You're makin' it tough on me, chief," Les managed to grin. "Yup, you saved my skin, awright, no doubt about it, and I'm much obliged to you, but it ain't easy to trust a guy in a Halloween mask. At least, it won't be for everybody else hereabouts, and that's a fact. Tarnation—I almost shot you a minute ago! Question is... do you believe you can trust me, too?"

The Skeleton nodded.

"I wouldn't have selected you if I didn't, and your trust would be impossible without my mask," he replied. "You're quite correct, of course. It'll be better if no one else knows of us. I assure you, there are far worse things coming to your town than stampeding saurians and invading alien arthropods. For now, that's all I can tell you. Will you cooperate?"

Sheriff Les lifted an eyebrow. He wanted to trust the costumed giant, and a small part of himself believed he could. If only he could get past the roadblock of that mask. It was so concealing, so sinister.

"Like to go along with you. I really would. Now, don't take this as an insult... but what happens if I refuse?"

The Skeleton lunged forward in a blur of motion, unbelievably panther-quick for his great size. He gripped the sheriff by the collar, effortlessly lifted, and bodily tossed him a dozen feet away as if weightless. Les thrashed awkwardly in the thicket and, red-faced, drew his heavy revolver.

A blinding shaft of sunlight beaming through the branches disrupted his aim, and the deafening shot went astray. After a couple rapid blinks, Les's vision cleared and he could finally see the loathsome creatures surrounding him.

"I tried to warn you! Your weapon is useless against them!" the Skeleton bellowed. "Stay in that sunbeam and you'll be safe!"

Les dropped to one knee, aghast at the vision of horror confronting him. A half dozen coal-black beasts, like massive hounds, ghoulishly gaunt and starved, with luminously frothing fangs, were encircling the sheriff and regarding him with ravenous red eyes.

Inexplicably, the splash of bright sunshine actually seemed to keep the fearsome predators at bay.

Despite the Skeleton's advice, Sheriff Les blasted away with his big Colt. Just couldn't help himself. He might have been shooting at smoke, for all its effect on the hell-hounds.

The giant flung himself into the savage pack. The full fury of the impact was horrible. Frightful guttural jaws snapped, ripping at the costume and flesh of their masked enemy. Terrific blows landed, nearly as loud as pistol shots. With the odds gravely against him the Skeleton fought fearlessly like a living dynamo. Les had never seen anything like it.

Suddenly, amid the flurry, one of the beasts was flung directly into the sunbeam. The hellhound convulsed and screamed, and in an instant was gone. The Skeleton slowly retreated, out-numbered for all his strength. The snarling things advanced, rabid revenge in their eyes, backing him against a huge obstructing willow. There was no place left to escape.

It happened almost too quickly to comprehend. The Skeleton gripped at the gnarled trunk and wrenched up in a sudden, impossible effort. The great tree was uprooted and swung as a club. The monstrous hounds scattered from the bone-bursting impact—and an even bigger, brighter stream of sunlight beamed freely onto the forest floor. Les stared mutely as the creatures writhed, whimpered, and melted into nothingness.

The Skeleton arose torn and bleeding, staggering toward him.

Les approached, wishing to help, but the offer was silently refused. He kept his distance, his brain flashing to that misty night at the Early Bird gas station and the horrible thing he'd witnessed. There was the memory of Dave Ross, too, his best friend of more than twenty years. Killed right before his eyes.

And now this masked giant had rescued him again. Les took a deep breath.

"You can count on me, chief," he promised at last. "Whatever you need. Where do we start?"

Somehow the skull mask had become even more grim, and the giant suddenly pointed over the sheriff's shoulder.

Les whirled, utterly astonished. Deep in the dim woods, fifty yards from them, stood a remarkable apparition. Horned and hideously hunched, clad in tatters and broken chains, it stared at them for a moment, and then vanished into the dark green murk.

When the sheriff turned back, he found that the Skeleton had also disappeared.

"Well, I'll declare..." Les murmured in a cold sweat. "There... there really is a Goat-Boy..."

"The Lost Circus"

"I DON'T believe it!" Molly's eyes adjusted to the dimness and widened, almost spellbound.

She couldn't completely wrap her mind around what she found inside the tent. Wonders abounded, from canvas ceiling to dirt floor, with dozens of miracles in every nook and corner. Most of the magic was in the form of softly glowing increscent globules, each containing different hazy moving pictures, all defying gravity, and hanging like fruit from an invisible tree. The weird, floating bubbles were being spewed from a deep green belching brew inside a big black cauldron. Once burped free, they swayed gently in mid-air, pulsing and growing as if alive.

"Just because you don't believe in something, doesn't mean it isn't real," Miss Grimalkin smiled, wagging a long finger. "Ahh... that one looks ripe—the one there in the corner. Could you pluck it for me, dearie?"

The luminous blob alluded Molly's timid grasp, but only for an instant, finally settling upon her finger-tips. It felt like slippery rubber, and possessed surprising heft. The thing grew rounder as the girl handled it, the fuzzy view of a deeply wooded forest interior slowly came into focus.

"What is this?" Molly grinned, fascinated, giving it to Miss Grimalkin.

"Why, it's a secret of course," the grey lady explained. "Now, don't pout, girl. I'm not keeping anything from you. I mean that this sphere itself is a secret, all of these—floating all around—they're all secrets, mysteries made solid, so that can be seen and solved."

She placed the globe upon an ornate copper base, suddenly sparkling into the form of a fortune-teller's crystal ball.

"It's an ancient recipe, brewing up secrets, and I'll admit I'm quite an expert," Miss Grimalkin said proudly. "It's quite true that Autumn came up with the idea and supplied the list of ingredients, but I mix the concoction so much better. Except for under very infrequent circumstances, she doesn't have thumbs, you see, so for all her cleverness she's a rather clumsy cat when it comes to cauldrons and kitchen work."

"You..." Molly whispered. "You... you're a... a..."

"A witch?" the old woman replied. "Yessiree, indeed I am. You might even say I'm *the* Witch. Yes, you might. Many others certainly would. My own modesty won't allow for such claims, however true they may be."

Molly took a wary step backward.

"Oh, don't look at me that way, Miss Molly," she chided with a grandmotherly grin. "It's not as if you're so very normal yourself, are you? Oh yes, I know your secret, too. At Autumn's suggestion, my cauldron told me all about you. You're a Fire Elemental. What? Didn't you realize that? Your body emits flame, ignited and fueled by your emotions. Have you yet discovered that you're also impervious to fire? Well, you are. There are many other wonderful things you can do, as well. You'll see soon enough. An impressive power, I'll grant you, but hardly unique. Oh, yes, there are others like you, and with even odder abilities. Autumn felt sure you'd be happier here. I hope you will give us a chance."

Molly was at a complete loss for words. It was all too much to process. Fire Elemental? Immune to flames? Real witches? And there were others, out there somewhere... even weirder...?

The girl peered into the crystal ball, its image alive and vibrant. "This is amazing..." she nearly giggled, more from nerves than humor.

"Why, yes, I suppose it is," the old woman nodded, frowning. "Of course, some secrets are more private than others. I can tell by that sudden yellow glow. Afraid I'd better look into this one by myself, my dear. Never fear, you'll find out when the time is right. Oh—Thurston? You still out there? Thurston?"

A tall, gangling figure staggered into the tent upon two legs that didn't bend the right way.

"Ah, lovely, there you are, Thurston," Miss Grimalkin spoke softly, as one might to a shy pet.

Molly gasped, getting a good look at him. Thurston could best be described as a man-sized sock-puppet, with shiny black button eyes and a brass zipper mouth.

"This is Thurston," the grey lady introduced him, and the awkward thing bowed. "He's a rag-golem, and is also the foreman of our carnival crew. Thurston sounds a bit strange, because his vocal cords are made from banjo strings, but he's much brighter than the rest of them and will show you around our little lost circus. Oh, don't be scared of him, dear. He's mostly made of cloth and a few dried pumpkin seeds, you could quite easily lift him off his cotton-stuffed feet and tear him to pieces, although that would only hurt his feelings. You're sure to become good friends. Thurston is one hundred percent dependable, aren't you, my boy? Now run along you two. I've got witch-work to do."

MOLLY STROLLED along with Thurston, who proved to be quite pleasant company, politely introducing her to the carnival chaotically created before her eyes. Dozens of rag-golems were on the job, hammering, sawing, painting, and raising the big tents, assembling the booths and rides, relentlessly and untiring. It was dizzying to watch, like seeing a cartoon brought to life, and the girl laughed out loud in spite of herself.

Thurston skewed his knitted head, conveying a sense of mortification. *Good grief*, Molly thought. *This boy has very tender feelings.*

"So, Thurston," she forced seriousness, "how long have you, uh, worked for Miss Grimalkin?"

"Worked...?" Thurston pondered, then the zipper-mouth curled. "Oh, I see what you mean, Miss. Well, I've been with her, in one form or another, for ages and ages. I don't pay much attention to clocks or calendars."

Molly again fought to suppress a giggle, but there was no use. The rag-golem's banjo-twanging speech was way beyond ridiculous. Thinking quickly, she changed her chuckle into a fake coughing fit.

"Oh my goodness gracious! Are you all right, Miss?" Thurston's concern peaked to a shrill, absolutely hilarious falsetto. "Is there anything I can do for you?"

The girl settled down, blushing with guilt.

"Suppose my throat's a bit dry, that's all. Never did have that tea Miss Grimalkin promised, y'know."

Without another word, although nodding spastically, Thurston promptly escorted Molly into a massive circus wagon, magnificently ornate with carved Jack O' Lantern faces, richly painted with bright oranges and glossy blacks. It was surprisingly spacious inside, somewhat garishly furnished with carefully preserved antiques possibly hundreds of years old, all dust-free and looking brand new. The rag-golem fumbled around for a minute in the cupboards, finally opened the little ice box door.

"I'm so sorry, Miss," he sounded heartbroken, "I'm very much afraid there isn't any tea, but we have a couple bottles of Gorilla Grape soda..."

"That'd be awesome."

"Very good, Miss. Now... where's that bottle opener?"

"It's okay, the cap twists off. See?"

"Well, I'll be dashed! Look at that! So they do! How clever!" Thurston was genuinely impressed.

As Molly sipped the fizzy purple soda, she examined a massive portrait, painted in oils, taking up most of the space on an interior wall. She immediately recognized Miss Grimalkin in the picture, and it was an excellent likeness except for the weird witch's costume she was wearing, including peaked hat, and broomstick, and the odd greenish-grey cast of her skin. Make-up, no doubt. The three figures posed along beside her were also dressed for Halloween. An especially ominous image of Autumn the black cat stared back from the portrait, too, with her unsettling yellow-green glare. She looked even more photo-real than the others.

"Thurston," Molly sniffed, the violet bubbles tickling her nose, "who're these guys? Weird, but—except for Miss Grimalkin and Autumn— I'm sure I've never seen them before, but somehow they look familiar."

There was a sudden tension, like static in the room. Even good-natured Thurston seemed apprehensive. He paused a full minute before answering.

"Ah, yes, very well, Miss," he was hesitant. "The gentleman wearing the shroud is, pardon me, I mean, was Sebastian Adams. He was always very kind to me, rest his soul. The other... the one in the Devil's costume... well, that was Arthur Van Blythe. The less said about him the better."

Well, that was intriguing. Molly had been fascinated by the red-cloaked image the instant she saw it, particularly the handsomely chiseled face beneath the horned cowl. There was a hint of humor playing upon the lips, but a cold fierceness in the black eyes which didn't quite seem to match.

"The bad boy of the group, huh?" Molly nodded . "I sure can pick 'em. But he's still kinda cool."

Thurston's button eyes looked mortified.

"Believe me, Miss Molly," he said aghast. "that was one thing he certainly was not."

Clearly it was time to change the subject. She turned back to the portrait, gazing at the fifth frightful figure.

"Who's the big bonehead in the skeleton suit?" she wondered.

"So, you're the one."

Molly whirled around at the rumbling voice behind her, confronting a costumed giant identical to the image in the picture.

"Um, hi," the girl looked upward, and kept looking up.

The Skeleton stood in the wagon's doorway, like an impassable monolith. Molly attempted a forced fake giggle.

"I was, uh, just asking about you."

"That will be all, Thurston," the giant's voice seethed with restrained power.

The jittery rag-man departed without a word, leaving Molly alone with the stranger. He glared at her with vicious yellow eyes, burning like lantern light.

"You're just a child," the Skeleton told her. "The Witch was wrong. Go home."

Her heart pounding with sudden panic, Molly didn't need to be told twice.

#

"The Evil Shadow"

IT WAS early evening, but seemed darker than it should. Sheriff Les Charles was looking forward to getting home, absently steering down lumpy, old coiling country back roads, completely lost in thought. A lot had happened in the past few hours and he was still struggling to wrap his brain around it. No luck, so far.

He didn't see the State Police patrol car following him, until it finally blasted a brief screech of its siren. Reluctantly, Les pulled over toward a briar-clustered patch. He groaned, glancing into the rearview mirror, recognizing State Trooper Dick Ashcraft swaggering out from his car.

"G'evenin', Sheriff," Ashcraft grinned, his dark glasses ablaze from the setting sun. "Can you depart from your vehicle, please?"

Les took a deep breath, letting it out in a huff. Swinging open the door, he sprang into the chilled breeze and fluttering leaves.

"What's the idea of shadowin' and squawkin' at me like that, Ashcraft? You coulda got me on the radio a lot quicker."

"Gettin' jittery, Sheriff?" Ashcraft spoke with a cinnamon toothpick stuck in his front teeth. "Or just plain feelin' guilty?"

Les's face grew hot as he took a firm step closer. Much as he'd tried, he never liked Ashcraft.

"What kinda crack is that?"

"Simmer down, Les," Trooper Ashcraft raised himself to his full impressive stature. "This ain't no game of Rook I'm drumming up here. It's official State Police business."

"Do tell?" Les felt a shudder. "A private meeting on a secluded road? Not very 'by-the-book' if you ask me."

"No one's askin' ya," Ashcraft's smirk drooped, "but I am tryin' to warn ya—as one ol' army buddy to another. Now, ya better think twice before shootin' yer mouth off again."

"Okay, that does it," Les turned back to his patrol car. "I just wanna get home, have my supper, and try to sleep more than two hours. Don't ever pull me over like this again."

"Hold your horses, Sheriff," the Trooper snarled. "Lemme make sure I got this right. Yer old boss was killed in a hit an' run, by an as-yet unidentified eighteen-wheeler. And they scraped 'im up, or what was left of 'im, off the road in front of the old Early Bird fillin' station. Stickin' to that story, are ya?"

Les whirled slowly, his gut clenched.

"That's the report I filed," Les retorted.

Ashcraft's frog-like smile split his mouth so widely that the toothpick dropped out.

"But it ain't what really happened, is it?" his ham-sized fist grabbed a plastic bag from his car. "A couple coon hunters found this snagged in a tree limb on Bee Knob Hill, half a mile from the Early Bird. Now, how in the world do ya think it got there?"

Les gaped at the sight of the bagged bundle in the Trooper's grip. His eyes blurred and his brain buzzed. It felt like a nightmare.

Trooper Ashcraft held the torn, bloody shirt and badge of Sheriff Dave Ross.

"IT WASN'T right for you to chase her away," Miss Grimalkin chided, stirring her cauldron.

The Skeleton turned aside, frowning under his mask.

"I didn't chase her," he grumbled defensively. "I simply told her to go home."

"Same thing and you know it," said the grey lady in quiet disgust. "Really, sometimes you forget how frightening you can be. Especially to someone so young and inexperienced as our Miss Molly."

The giant rose to his feet, the top of his massive head scrapping the tent's ceiling.

"That's exactly my point. The girl's only a child. She doesn't belong here," he attempted to sound detached and aloof.

Miss Grimalkin stepped away from her bubbling brew, shaking her wooden spoon at him.

"That's not for you to say," she affirmed. "Never was. Of course, the girl belongs here with us, or Autumn would not have chosen her."

"The cat is wrong," he shrugged.

"Autumn has never been wrong."

"She was this time."

The grey woman couldn't help but smile.

"She wasn't wrong about *you*."

The giant froze. Only his shallow breathing betrayed him as other than a chiseled black-and-while effigy. Sadly, he bowed his great head.

"Oh, my dear old friend," the witch said softly, eyes moist and shining. "The girl is so much like you."

"She is nothing like me. No one is like me."

"But she is. Molly's alone, abandoned, and scared. She's been thrown away by people who were supposed to take care of her and protect her. Just like you were. And like I was, too. Don't you see? We're all outsiders. The poor thing is only starting to discover herself, her true self. Unlike what happened to us, we can help her so she doesn't feel quite so strange and so alone. Besides, she has nowhere else to go. She's bright, brave, and wants to do good. And she has an incredible power that needs to be controlled, or the girl could become a deadly danger to everyone. Molly Aldrich belongs here as much as anyone ever could."

The black cat slinked into the tent, hopped effortlessly to a tabletop and curled up in repose. She offered the Skeleton a rather nasty stare, but he'd already turned away from her.

"You're right about one thing," the giant admitted. "I scared the girl. I regret that."

Miss Grimalkin tip-toed, giving his masked chin a gentle caress.

"There's a way to fix it, you know."

He nodded slowly.

"You're right about that, too."

And the Skeleton vanished outside, into the deepening dusk.

"LET'S TALK turkey," State Trooper Ashcraft dangled the bloody bag of rags, "Y'know, I don't necessarily hafta hand this over to my superiors…"

Sheriff Charles fumed.

"Spit it out, Ashcraft. What do you want?"

"I'm sure you've already guessed, Les, ol' pal," he grinned like an alligator. "First thing, I wanna see you resign. Say it's because of your health. Your wife and kids are worried over you. I don't care what excuse you use. Then, you contact the governor and convince him to appoint me as Sheriff of Woodland. I'll keep your filthy little secret—whatever it is—and I'll take over your duties. Then, we'll both go on with our lives. Whaddaya say?"

"You know where you can go," Les suggested.

Ashcraft's bloated eyes bugged with temper.

"Look, man, you know that me and Breezy Busso deserved to win that election a lot more than you and Dave."

"I know what you deserve, awright."

"Think you're so smart, don'tcha?" the Trooper flourished the plastic sack again, like a trump card. "Truth is I don't much care what happened to ol' Dave. Maybe it all happened like what you scribbled down in that report. Maybe a coon found this bloody piece of uniform at the side of the road and dragged it up into that tree. I doubt it, though. Whatever the truth is, I'm bettin' you're hidin' it to protect yourself. So, how about it? Just do like I say and we can go our separate ways, both full of respect and dignity."

State Trooper Dick Ashcraft was five years younger, eight inches taller, and forty pounds heavier than Les. None of that kept the sheriff trudging forward, balling up his fists.

"I'll show you what you're full of," he steamed.

"Help! Police! Murder!"

Both men spun at the shrill scream. A dark-haired teenage girl scuttled up toward them from across the gravel road, pausing breathlessly at the Sheriff's fender.

"Take it easy," Les said. "Calm down. A few deep breaths. That's it."

"What're you doin' all the way out here in the sticks? What's this all about?" Ashcraft barked.

Molly panted and coughed, some of the color returning to her cheeks.

"Well…" she gasped, not quite as realistically as she'd planned, "There was this accident. Two trucks. Big smash. They flipped over. It's terrible."

"Thought you said there was a murder?" the Trooper jutted out his paunchy chin.

The girl nodded somewhat overly enthusiastically.

"That's right! After they crashed, two guys crawled out of their wrecked trucks and starting cussing and slugging away at each other! Sure looked like bloody murder to me!"

Trooper Ashcraft grimaced with suspicion.

"Awright, then. Sounds mighty fishy to me, but I suppose we oughta check it out. C'mon, Les…"

Molly suddenly stepped between them, her doe eyes imploring to Les.

"What about me?" she went full-out drama diva. "I'm already late and I'll be in an awful lot of trouble. It's not my fault those dumb old trucks crashed. Can't you drive me home?"

"Now, look here, young lady…" Ashcraft wanted to argue, still suspicious of her.

"She's right," Sheriff Les interrupted. "A road accident is a job for the State Police. You go check it out, and I'll get her home. I'm sure her folks are worrying themselves sick."

Ashcraft hedged a moment, and then stomped back toward his car.

"Awright, I'll go," he growled. "We'll finish our little dance later… Sheriff."

"Don't start without me," Les agreed, and he and Molly watched the tail lights until they disappeared around a wooded curve in the road.

"Quick! We gotta go!" she gripped the sheriff firmly on the sleeve.

"Wha—where are we going?" Les startled.

"Anywhere!" Molly suggested, pulling him toward the squad car. "There's no wrecks! No murders! I made it all up! Quick! Run for our lives!"

CHAPTER TEN
"Freddy-Fright Finds a Friend"

THE DAY had been full of surprises.

First, Molly had seen a ghost. It wasn't her imagination, she was quite certain of that. The apparition haunting the dim dank basement of *Aunt Ethel's Melon Patch Diner* was as real and scary as a bad report card. No doubt about it.

Next, a spooky-smart black cat had led her thirty miles to meet a witch. Molly wasn't being disrespectful by thinking of her as a witch, in fact, the gentle grey lady had openly admitted that fact. And proudly.

Then, there was that man made of rags. And he was alive. At least, he walked and talked. That should have been pretty creepy under other circumstances, but he was really more funny, even sort of endearing, than anything else.

There had been the giant in the skeleton suit, too. Thinking of him still gave her the shivers.

Lastly, after a brief rather scurried explanation in the patrol car, Molly was pleasantly surprised to learn that kindly Aunt Ethel, who'd fed her breakfast for free, and had even offered her a job at the diner, was the sheriff's wife. And, before she knew it, she was seated at the table with the whole family, shoveling down big heaping spoonfuls of hot home-made potato soup like nobody's business.

Aunt Ethel politely excused herself from the table to get some fresh pears from the backyard tree for dessert. Les followed after her, mumbling about stretching his legs. Molly scarcely noticed, completely absorbed by tall-tales told by teenage Charlotte and her nine year old brother, Barry.

"I'm awful glad to have her here, Les," Aunt Ethel said, once they were out of ear-shot. "She's a sweet little thing. Feel sort of sorry for her. I'm betting she's not as old as she acts. Probably a little younger than Charlotte. Pretty sure she's a runaway, but she won't say much about herself."

"Yup, that's what I'm figuring, too. She's sure a strange one. I'll talk to her more after supper, find out where she belongs and get her home," Les nodded.

"I don't see why she lied to bad ol' Dick Ashcraft. That could put her in a heap of trouble."

Les scratched his head.

"Not if he can't find her, it won't—and I'll make sure he don't," he replied thoughtfully, almost thinking out loud. "I dunno, she said she just happened upon me and Ashcraft having our... uh... difference of opinion. She thought we were gonna start to scuffle and took it upon herself to break it up. I asked her why it was any of her business, and she just said it was the right thing to do."

"That's pretty bold!" Aunt Ethel laughed. "Lucky she took your side. Wonder how come?"

Les grinned, shaking his head.

"I asked her that, too. A sheriff is sorta like a detective, y'know. She told me she could tell a no-account creep when she saw one, or somethin' like that, and she didn't think it was fair that Ashcraft is so much bigger than me. Plus, she said I had an 'honest face'."

"Well, you do, darlin'," Aunt Ethel smooched his rough cheek. "What did dumb ol' Dick want with you, anyways?"

Les lost his grin, busying himself picking pears.

"Not worth mentionin'. You know that crazy ol' jackass."

Meanwhile, at the supper table, Charlotte's talk had turned to spooks.

"...so our brother Marion—he's away in the Marines—collected a zillion lightning bugs in mason jar, and went running—wild as the devil—with that jar held high over his head through Monk Whelan's okra patch, whooping and hollering to beat the band! Well, old Monk—he's the one who disappeared from the Early Bird filling station, don'tcha know—thought for sure that his old dead grandmamma had come out of her grave to haunt him for planting okra instead of rhubarb! He wet his overalls right there on his front porch!"

Molly hadn't laughed so hard in a long time. Felt really good. Charlotte was very funny, with a seemingly unending series of sagas to tell, all of them with a laugh-out-loud punch-line. Barry was quiet company, but the phony spook story caused him to grimace and his sister took quick notice of it.

"Of course," Charlotte started, her grey eyes dancing, "that's nothing compared to ol' Freddy-Fright! Right, Barry?"

Barry had become suddenly very studious of the last pea on his plate, jabbing for it over and over with his fork, without success.

"I dunno," he mumbled.

"Freddy—who?" Molly wondered.

"Ah, ol' Freddy-Fright is something else. Barry's seen him lots of times. Y'see, Freddy is a—wait. Barry oughta tell you about Freddy-Fright himself."

Barry gave up on spearing the pea, squashing it.

"I don't wanna, Charlotte."

"Okay, then," Charlotte winked at Molly. "But tell me if I make a mistake. You see, Freddy-Fright is a ghost that haunts the basement of mom's diner. Didn't she tell you about it? Anyway, sometimes—Barry says—Freddy-Fright shows up in our barn, too. How many times have you seen him now, Barry? Four or five times?"

Molly felt a chill, remembering her experience that morning.

"You've really seen him?" she grinned at the boy, but wasn't laughing.

He nodded, looking a little pale.

"Sure I have... 'cept nobody believes me."

Charlotte snickered a bit, winked again at Molly, then tried to behave herself.

"Heck, I believe you, Barry," Molly admitted. "How do you know his name? Have you talked to him?"

The boy shifted a bit in his chair, shooting a sharp look at his sister. She was going to crack up any minute, he just knew it.

"He was a kid in my class. Freddy had these big buck teeth. We all kinda laughed at him. Carrie Beam said Freddy's teeth prolly glowed in the dark. Everybody called him 'Freddy-Fright'. That tornado last year killed him and his whole family. Guess Freddy's come back to get even. Wish he knew how sorry I am."

Molly nodded thoughtfully, and gave Barry a playful tug on the bill of his baseball cap.

"Tell you what, kiddo. Next time I see Freddy, how about if I apologize for you?"

"Really?" his eyes lit up. "You'd really do that?"

Charlotte wrestled to control a giggle, while Molly gazed seriously out the kitchen window.

"Sure thing," she affirmed, looking at the dark old barn. "You bet I will."

IT WAS sometime after 2 a.m. when Molly sneaked out of the farmhouse from her warm spot on the soft living room couch. She'd waited until everyone was long asleep, especially Sheriff Les, who'd been snoring away for over a half hour. He'd stayed up late with her, barraging her with tons of questions, and her tight-lipped stubbornness had utterly exhausted him. Finally, the sheriff had given up, shaking his head sadly, and saying a social worker would get to the bottom of things in the morning.

Nope, Molly decided. *That's not gonna happen.*

Still, the girl knew she couldn't leave without at least attempting to keep her promise to Barry. Even in their short amount of time together Molly grew to like the family very much, and she thought she'd figured out a way to repay their kindness. Besides, she was still more than a bit ashamed at her cowardice in the basement of the diner.

Tightly clenching her small fists, Molly swallowed hard and warily walked toward the looming black barn.

The weathered barn door groaned as Molly narrowly opened it, squeezing herself within. It seemed like a silent immense cathedral inside, as frosty moonlight shimmered between warped boards glistening off the haystacks. Oddly, she suddenly saw the puffs of her breath. It was a lot colder in the barn than outside.

Molly held up her hand, a cool blue flame danced on her open palm like a living lantern. She had to carefully concentrate, as there was a lot of dry hay around her, but she needed the illumination. A sad muted voice muttered immediately.

"Can you find my momma?"

The girl turned around slowly. Yup. It was the Ghost, all right.

He stood there small and timid, draped in a worn bed sheet, just like before, staring scared out from the unevenly cut eyeholes.

When Molly's flickering flame neared the apparition, he seemed to lose a sense of solidity in its light, fading into a glow of milky translucence.

"Hi there, Freddy," she knelt down to his level, fighting her fear. "I'm Molly. Remember me?"

"Uh-huh," the bed-sheet nodded.

Molly noticed that Freddy's semi-transparent grass-stained sneakers didn't quite touch the dirt floor. It was very freaky. She hoped her goose-bumps didn't show up in the dim light of her flame.

"Um… listen," Molly stammered slightly, "do you remember a boy named Barry at your school?"

"His desk was in the row next to mine," the Ghost replied.

"Right. Well… Barry says that sometimes he might not have been very nice to you. Didn't mean to hurt your feelings. He wants you to know that he's very sorry."

There was cold silence for a moment.

"That's okay," Freddy answered, almost absently.

"Cool," Molly smiled. "Whatcha doing out here in the barn, all by yourself?"

The Ghost hovered higher, rotating left, then right. There was an obvious air of anxiety emanating from him. He truly looked lost.

"Can you find my mamma? I've looked all over."

Molly's smile melted into soft sadness, knowing what she had to do.

"Well, okay," her eyes grew damp. "Suppose now's as good a time to tell you as any. C'mon over here and sit with me… uh, if you can sit."

Freddy drifted closer to the girl.

"You know where Mamma is?"

"Yeah… I mean, no. I mean… I'm just not sure how to tell you."

"Is it something bad?"

"It is, yeah. Remember that storm, Freddy? The really awful one?"

"Uh-huh. Saw it blow the tractor into the pond and the henhouse went straight up in the sky. Wind broke all our windows. Whole house was shaking. Sounded like a train rolling across the roof. Real scary. I was trying to find Mamma. Then, I think… I fell asleep."

Tears rolled off Molly's quivering chin. Her lips parted, but she could say nothing. The Ghost floated close enough to lightly touch her arm, feeling much like a slight static tingle.

"I died, didn't I?"

Molly nodded, wishing she could hold him.

"Mamma and Papa, too?"

"Afraid so."

His blue eyes dimmed behind the sheet.

"Oh."

He glided aimlessly in slow circles for a few minutes, then turned to her.

"What about Lady? She's my dog. Have you see her running around?"

"Can't say I have," the girl reluctantly shook her head.

"But why?" Freddy sobbed slightly. "If we was all kill'd, then why ain't Mamma and Papa and Lady here, too?"

That was actually a really good question. Molly pondered it for a few seconds.

"I don't know," she admitted gently.

The two remained in silence for awhile. Crickets started chirping again for the first time since Molly had entered the barn, their repetitive rhythm adding a sort of earthy warmth that was missing before. Finally, Freddy raised his sheet-shrouded head.

"Wonder why I'm still in my Trick 'r Treat outfit?" he mumbled, examining his glowing ectoplasmic hands. "Guess I'm really kinda lucky."

Molly liked the change in his voice, calmer and less scared.

"Yeah? Whatcha mean, Freddy?"

"Well, nothing can ever hurt me… so that's pretty cool. And I guess can't die again."

"Yup, that *is* pretty cool," the girl beamed a smile.

She was really starting to like this timid little specter.

"So, what should I do, Molly?," he wondered. "Where am I suppose to go now?"

Suddenly, both realized they weren't alone. The gigantic figure of the Skeleton emerged from the shadows.

"Come with me," his voice droned low, like a distant storm. "It's not safe here."

Freddy glanced up at Molly. She smiled and nodded.

"Where are we going, Mr. Skeleton?" he inquired frankly. "Are there any dogs?"

The Skeleton tilted his skull head.

"No... but there's a cat. Now keep quiet. Let's move."

Concealed among the bushes and ivy, suspicious eyes secretly spied from the edge of the woods. An ominous, costumed giant, a teenage girl who's bare hand smoldered like a burning torch, and a incandescent glob stealthily exited the barn to be abruptly swallowed into the great labyrinth of the cornfield beyond, rapidly vanishing as if they'd been figments of the spy's imagination.

State Trooper Dick Ashcraft fearfully lowered his binoculars with trembling hands.

"Countdown to Chaos"

SHERIFF LES Charles left for work much too early. Still dead-tired, Aunt Ethel worriedly walked him to his squad car.

"I wish you'd let me fix you some breakfast," she offered.

"No time," he winced, glancing at his watch. "Got to find that girl. I shoulda known she'd be gone this morning. Stupid of me."

"Don't be too rough on her," Aunt Ethel implored. "I feel she's had some great trouble. I liked her, Les. Liked her a lot. Help her, if you can."

"I will," Les promised. "Better be goin', hon. If Ashcraft finds her first—well, it won't be good."

MOLLY WAS gobbling down her second stack of buttery banana waffles, while guzzling a quart of orange juice to wash them down. The Witch shook her grey head in wonder. For such a little thing, Molly could sure pack it away.

"Mss Grrmllknnn… whss tht pichr allbot?" the girl inquired with her mouth half full.

"This portrait?" the Witch pondered the framed picture for a moment. "Ah, this was painted in the old days, when our little group was still together. Haven't you seen us before? Don't we look familiar to you?"

Molly swallowed, nodding.

"Sort of like grown-up Trick 'r Treaters, to tell you the truth."

The grey lady grinned, then became wistful.

"Indeed," her gaze grew cloudy. "We prowled the world, perhaps *patrolled* might be a better word, seeking out the wickedest, most terrible threats imaginable. We sought them out and we fought them. Our myth still continues, when children dress up as witches, black cats, skeletons, ghosts, and devils and haunt the avenues on Halloween night—to scare away the other scary things. The bad things. For us, it was for real."

Downing another forkful, Molly slurred through the maple syrup.

"Whup… happen'd to … the udder two guyss… in duh pichure?" she hadn't been able to get them out of her head.

"Fallen soldiers, I'm afraid," Miss Grimalkin said softly. "Old friends long lost. It's a dangerous world out there, as you've already seen for yourself. Sometimes I wonder why we've risked so much for people who would hate us, probably want to destroy us, if they knew we lived among them."

"Heck, I know why," Molly asserted, matter of-factly. "You guys did it 'cause no one else could. Kinda like a 'Halloween Legion.' It was the right thing to do."

The Witch stared stunned at the munching teenager. The girl understood without being told. She was even more amazing than the grey lady had already believed.

Molly was chewing a final cheek-full as Thurston came waggling into the wagon, leaving a carefully wrapped scarlet-colored bundle of fabric on the breakfast table.

"Ah, Thurston! It's done, then? Just the right color, too! How wonderful! Well done! Well done!" the Witch girlishly clapped her hands.

"G'morning, Thurston," Molly waved at the rag-man. "Real tasty waffles."

Thurston dramatically bowed in his sincere, but awkward manner.

"I'm very happy you found them enjoyable, Miss," he bleated in his banjo twang. "Now, if you'll excuse me, I have three hundred forty-seven other chores that require my urgent attention to before our Big Night. Busy! Busy! Busy!"

"Uh, 'Big Night'…?" Molly asked, after Thurston had departed.

"Why, yes, of course!" the Witch beamed. "Our Creepy Crawly Carnival of Chaos opens tonight—and one night only! Free admission for anyone with a pulse! Not for the squeamish! Fun and Frights for all! Tonight is *Halloween*!"

Molly giggled at the grey lady's ambulant antics. She seemed mad as a hatter sometimes. With a flourish of extra exuberance she tossed the red bundle unto the girl's lap.

"For me?" Molly was taken by surprise.

"Presumptuous of me, I know," the Witch nodded, "but you'll need something appropriate to wear tonight. Don't worry, it will fit you perfectly. Thurston is one hundred percent dependable at the sewing machine—as he is with everything else. Why don't you try it on behind my dressing screen? I'll drag out my old mirror so you can have a better look at yourself."

Molly did as suggested, and rather excitedly so. She didn't know how long it had been since she'd had anything new. Most of her clothes she'd made herself. Miss Grimalkin was absolutely right, the crimson outfit fit her like a glove. It was perfectly perfect. In every way. Suddenly, for some weird reason, she felt she was going to cry.

"This is so cool," she breathed. "Okay, ready or not, here I come!"

The girl was startled for a second, stepping from behind the dressing screen. A strange, wondrously beautiful young woman stood in front of her, but then Molly saw it was only an illusion reflected in a great ornately framed mirror. It wasn't her own reflection. The lovely image belonged to the Witch.

"The trouble with mirrors," the grey lady told her, "is they sometimes reflect too much. Ignore it, and come closer to see yourself."

"B-but… how…?"

"My reflection is merely part of the price for my power, don't let it trouble you, child. We'll talk about it later. This is your moment. Come closer, take a look at yourself."

"You mean," Molly gasped, "you really look like… like that? You're so beautiful…"

With an impatient eye-roll the Witch adjusted the angle of the mirror, and Molly saw herself full length for the first time, a blaze of bright red, from her horned hood, to her shiny scarlet boots.

"Wowza. I'm hotsy-totsy."

"Ha-ha-ha—! Is that all you've got to say?"

Miss Grimalkin laughed as the girl hugged her till her ribs ached.

"Thank you… thank you so much. I wanna go show Freddy and Bone-Head—uh, I mean the skeleton guy."

"Freddy's outside playing with Autumn, Careful, he's a bit difficult to see in direct sunlight. As for 'Bone-head'… heh-heh-heh… I rather like that… try the big black tent, that's the laboratory. He tends to brood there a lot."

"M'kay! Seeya later!"

Like a racing red comet, Molly dashed from the wagon to find her new friends. Suddenly alone, the grey lady dabbed a tear from her cheek with a lacy silk hanky.

"What a dear little thing she is... so sweet... so wise," the Witch murmured. "Such a good little Devil."

"**H**EYA. WHATCHA doing?" Molly poked her horned, hooded head into the black tent flap.

The Skeleton stood working among a complex mass of electronic gadgetry, flicking switches and turning knobs.

"I'm working," he replied, without turning around.

Glass tubes hummed, pulsing with light and color. Spidery crackles of electricity leaped from pole to pole. It was all really quite impressive.

"Very cool. Looks like a Frankenstein movie, or something," tiny blue sparks danced in her brown eyes. "Mind if we come in?"

Abruptly, the giant switched off the machines.

"If you wish. I'm finished, anyway."

Molly stepped inside with Freddy, who instantly changed from cellophane to solid within the gloom of the tent. Autumn followed behind them, making herself comfortable upon a tabletop to began her morning bath.

"So... whaddaya think? Like it?" Molly twirled like a ballerina, her slinging spiked tail striking an empty glass beaker to the floor. "Uh... sorry."

"A bit early for you to be in costume, isn't it?" he murmured, ignoring the broken glass.

"Heh," she smirked. "Look who's talking. I'll bet you probably sleep in yours."

The giant swung around to her.

"What do you mean?" he glared down.

"Well, let's face it, I've never seen you wearing anything else. Don'tcha ever take it off?"

"No."

"Seriously?"

"Quite."

"Not even to wash it?"

"That doesn't deserve an answer."

"Not even just the mask?"

"Not even."

"Isn't it hot?"

"It's fine."

"And you don't ever take it off?"

"Never."

"Why?"

"Because I don't."

"That's no reason."

"Skip it."

Freddy had drifted among the control panel, immensely cluttered and complicated.

"Excuse me, sir," he asked meekly. "Did you build all this yourself?"

"Most of it," the giant admitted. "That is, I constructed it according to Autumn's conception as translated by Grimalkin."

Molly smiled at the cat.

"Y'know, if you had thumbs, we'd all be in trouble."

Autumn paused in her grooming, giving the girl a sour look.

"What kinda work were you doing, sir?" the Ghost wondered.

The Skeleton frowned, trying his best to be patient. Especially with Autumn in the room.

"I was broadcasting a carnival advertisement to all the radio and television stations," he explained curtly.

"Oh yeah," Molly mused. "I saw that cool TV commercial a couple nights ago. 'See live monsters! See real ghosts! Guys—bring your girlfriends! Girls—see if your boyfriends are men or mice!' Hah! With free admission, I'll bet just about everyone in Woodland will show up."

"That's the idea," the Skeleton nodded. "We can protect them better here. The carnival is the safest place they can be tonight."

The girl's eyes bugged.

"What's gonna happen tonight?"

"Didn't the Witch tell you?"

"Nope."

"Then, let's change the subject," the giant turned away.

Molly made a face at him behind his back.

Wowza. Whadda crabby cuss.

"Heya, I have another question—" she began.

"Oh no…"

"Don't be so cross. I'm just trying to get to know you."

"Go ahead," he sighed.

"Well," the girl began keeping count on her fingers, "Autumn's really spooky-smart, Miss Grimalkin does magic spells, Freddy can float, be invisible, and go through walls and stuff, I make fire… what do you do? I mean, I know you're really strong and all that, but do you have any real supernatural powers?"

The silence lasted so long Molly was starting to think she wasn't going to get an answer at all. At last, the giant spoke with his head bowed.

"I have… one power."

"Cool beans! Can you show me?"

"To the contrary, I hope I never need to use it again."

"Huh—? How cuz?"

"Because it hurts."

There was such a profound sadness in his last three words Molly was struck speechless, a very rare moment, indeed. The silence simmered and ballooned within the tent until it felt ready to burst.

Suddenly, the door-flap opened wide, flooding in the daylight. The group whirled as a long shadow cast inside.

"So there you are!" Sheriff Les Charles was quite perturbed. "Had some funny feeling I'd might find you here, young lady. What in the world is goin' on here?!"

"So nice to see you again, Sheriff," Miss Grimalkin had slipped soundlessly inside behind him.

The grey lady was now costumed as Molly had seen her in the old painting, complete with tall peaked hat and a broomstick. She'd scrubbed away the thick pancake make-up from her face, too, uncovering its unnatural greenish-grey tint. Miss Grimalkin was the very image of a classic Halloween witch, as seen in a zillion old pictures and decorations.

"My spell lured you here a bit quicker than I'd planned, my boy, but now that you're here you might as well have a seat and lend an ear. And hold onto your hat. I'm going to spill the whole scary story…"

CHAPTER TWELVE
"The Halloween Horror"

SHERIFF LES rubbed the back of his neck. Another headache was coming on, a real beaut. He'd been listening to Miss Grimalkin tell him of their troubles, non-stop, for hours. Oh, she'd been quite detailed and very thorough, he had to admit, but there was still so much he didn't understand.

"I might seem stupid, but what th' heck's a 'Phooka', anyway?" he asked, slipping back out of his squad car after signing off on the radio.

The little group of weirdos—as Les had come to think of them—including Molly, had followed him into the carnival parking area. Dozens of rag-golems, expertly directed by Thurston, scuttled about all over the grounds, fine-tuning the rides, firing up the food grills, and completing a hundred other blurry, dizzying chores. It was a disturbingly comical sight. Freddy wafted about in the brisk autumn breeze, becoming more visible each minute from the sinking evening sun, which added considerably to the sheriff's mounting anxiety.

"A Phooka," the Witch explained, "is an elemental entity of the woods, very rare in this country. In fact, in all my time in America I've only known of one other. Their spore is unmistakable. A Phooka is definitely what we are dealing with. They are shape-shifters who usually take the form of animals, often more than one at a time, always very large, and sometimes quite terrifying."

Les scratched at a raw place on his scalp.

"I dunno… this is all so tough to swallow…"

"Is a Phooka any more unlikely than *us*?" the Skeleton asserted. "Trust your own eyes. You've encountered the creature's magic numerous times already."

Sheriff Les nodded, and shuddered.

"Okay… awright… but what's this thing got against us? What did we ever do to it?"

"That's the puzzle," Miss Grimalkin admitted. "Phooka's can be trouble-makers, but they aren't vicious."

"Not vicious!" Les fumed. "The blamed thing has menaced the countryside! Scarin' little old ladies into heart attacks, almost rippin' me to pieces, and stompin' my best friend to death! This ain't no storybook fairy playin' jokes on folks—it's some of kinda monster!"

"Monsters are what the world has made of them, Sheriff," the Skeleton sadly grumbled.

"Y'know, maybe the Phooka is sick or something," Molly suggested, "and doesn't know what it's doing?"

"We could ask Harold, if we can find 'im. He lives in th' woods, too. Maybe he knows where the Poo-key is," Freddy shyly chimed in.

Molly startled, turning to the Ghost.

"Huh—? Who's 'Harold', Freddy?"

"He was my friend," he shrugged beneath the sheet. "Back when I was, uh, alive, Harold used to scratch on my window screen at night. I'd play records and read to him from my dinosaur books. Snuck snacks outside for him, too, until Mamma caught me and made me stop."

Sheriff Les felt queasy in the stomach.

"Sounds like the dat-blasted Goat-Boy to me!"

The black cat meowed and the Witch nodded.

"Freddy, did your friend seem ill or hurt?" she wondered.

The Ghost's shrouded head tilted.

"Not 'specially," he replied. "But he didn't like our barn, 'cuz there was spiders... and he was awful skeered of th' huntin' dogs, too."

"The weird spiders, spook-hounds, and that dinosaur you mentioned, Sheriff, this is all coming together," the grey lady rubbed her pointed chin. "Even the name 'Harold' makes sense. Phookas are sometimes the *heralds* of impending doom."

"This is even bigger than we feared," the Skeleton warned.

"And being Halloween, that will add considerably to its power," the Witch agreed. "Freddy, we have to find your friend and stop him. If we don't, he's going to hurt more people. Do you understand?"

The Ghost nodded.

"Sure don't want nobody hurt."

"Good boy. Can you tell us where Harold lives? Where does he hide?"

"Well... I used to let 'im sleep in th' cellar when it was cold... Mamma never knew, she wouldn't have liked that... but he hides out on Bee Knob Hill most of the time, I reckon. Dunno. He didn't ever say much."

Abruptly, a flurry of scarlet and orange leaves crawled right up to the Witch. She bent low as they whispered to her their secrets. At least some of their news was good.

"The crowds are arriving at our carnival," she announced. "They'll be safer here among us, and anything unusual anyone may witness will seem like merely part of the show, just as Autumn planned. Sheriff, have you successfully quarantined the Woodland community as she suggested?"

Les glanced down at the cat. She blinked back confidently.

"Uh, well, I've radioed in for temporary deputies, mostly my brothers and a couple cousins, and they're settin' up roadblocks,"

Les said. "Told 'em to make up some escaped convict story, if anyone got nosy. Nobody's gettin' in or out of Woodland tonight."

The Witch looked over her grey shoulder at the last rosy rays of sunlight melting behind Bee Knob Hill, looming darkly upon the horizon.

"Excellent! Our guests have come," she grinned grimly at a multitude of headlights spilling brightly over the carnival grounds. "Take your positions as planned, and make sure everyone leaves here alive after *midnight*."

Molly's eyes burnished as bright as the moon, flames dancing from her fingertips.

"Okay, hot-stuff," she murmured to herself, "let's see what I'm really made of."

SHERIFF LES and his deputies patrolled the back-roads and hollows. Strange sights stirred from the corners of their eyes, a creeping blackness keeping pace with their vehicles. Something massive seemed to move alongside them, slithering eel-like though the woods and cornfields.

Les glanced at his watch and groaned. At midnight the danger would be over, the old witch had said.

Couldn't come fast enough for him.

THE EXCITED crowds poured in, flooding the snack shacks and the sideshows. Scramblers, Carousels, and Tilt-a-Whirls spun wild, with the Ferris Wheel joyously jam-packed with passengers. Colorfully costumed kids raced from booth to booth, their pillow cases plumping with wax fangs, candy corn, and chocolate skulls, provided by Thurston and the other rag-men. Nobody stopped to question. Nobody thought this was anything but another fun Halloween.

The Witch, the Ghost, Molly in her Devil's suit, and the black cat, all walked among them, almost unnoticed. Ever watchful for trouble, they still couldn't help but be caught up, just a little bit, in the seasonal celebration. It was a brief, precious moment for the weird little group. Blending in with the crowd, they almost felt as if they fit in.

Molly was the first to see Autumn's ebony hackles rise, punctuated by a throaty hiss.

"Um... I think something's wrong. Do you feel it? The ground's starting to shake!"

"I'd hoped it wouldn't come to this," the Witch answered, "but we're ready."

The girl nervously glanced around them.

"Heya! What happened to Bone-Head?" she cried, aghast.

"He knows what to do," the grey lady affirmed. "And he's done it. Behold!"

It descended like an orange sun, a black painted face smirking above the cheering and applauding crowd. A great Jack O' Lantern hot air balloon glided effortlessly through the leaf-strewn air, with the giant figure of the Skeleton as pilot in the basket. Dipping low, he grasped Molly's hand hauling her on board as if she were a feather. Autumn leaped into the basket after the girl. Freddy floated along following them.

"No!" Molly shouted down to the grey lady. "I don't wanna leave you!"

"Don't fret, child!" the Witch called back. "I still have a few tricks up my sleeve!"

The girl glared at the giant.

"Stop it! I'm not a baby!" she snarled. "Stop trying to protect me! Something awful is gonna happen down there—and I wanna help!"

"You're getting your chance," the Skeleton pointed a bone-painted finger.

Molly turned and stared, saucer-eyed.

"Wowza…"

To the clapping guests below, this was the greatest Spook Show any of them had ever experienced. Amazing! Spectacular! Phenomenal!

But they hadn't seen anything yet…

A trio of titanic thundering Brontosaurs suddenly emerged from the darkness, stampeded their three hundred tons toward the carnival crowd.

CHAPTER THIRTEEN
"The Deadly Dreamer"

"OH MY goodness! They look so real!"

"Bravo! Bravo!"

"Mommy, I'm scared!"

"Relax! They're puppets, I'll bet! Just giant puppets on wires!"

"This is so cool!"

"Somebody smells like rotten broccoli!"

"Yuck!"

"Lemme outta here!"

"Holy Moley—what a show!"

The carnival crowd didn't know whether to cheer or to run, so most did both. Good thing, too, but no one was quick enough. Like raging locomotives, the prehistoric nightmares were nearly upon them.

"Those people are going to be trampled! Do something!" Skeleton boomed in the balloon basket.

"Like what—?!" Molly cried. "Th-those are dinosaurs! Dinosaurs—for cryin' out loud! I'm just a girl!"

"No! You're more than that! Now quickly—before they get closer to the crowd!"

Autumn's growled, glaring fiercely at the girl.

Molly bit her lip, her brain racing.

Awright... awright. Got it. Just might work.

"If I can distract them..." she concentrated, flame streaming from her hand. "...maybe we can lead them away!"

The plume of fire, pulsing like a thing alive, radiated flare intensity. The giant reptiles slowed, their small snakish eyes dazzled by the sudden brilliance.

"It... it's working!" Molly gritted her teeth. "We got their attention—but now what?!"

"Perhaps, they'll follow us away. How long can you maintain the flame?" the Skeleton bellowed.

"How the heck should I know?!" the girl shouted back. "I've never done anything like this before!"

Autumn sprang to Molly's shoulder, nudging her attention. Something even weirder was happening below. Breathlessly, the giant and the girl watched with the cat, as the three saurians began to tremble and collapse, erupting upon themselves in a screeching geyser of scales and sinew. They melted, blended, and transformed, merging from three behemoths into a lone leviathan, an enormous tentacled thing, expanding by the moment, until its gelatinous mountainous mass blotted out the moonlight.

Molly turned a bit green.

"I... think I'm gonna be sick," she gasped.

A few among the crowd fled in panic, but most had utterly hushed, frozen in fascination. The monstrous colossus seethed across the midway, its tentacles writhing through the abandoned rides and empty sideshows. Finally, the greasy grey feelers found the Ferris Wheel.

Twin screams harmonized, forty feet up, as the oozing tentacles coiled through the support spokes. Two terrified passengers had been trapped at the top, with no way down except to jump. With a great grinding wail, the heavy steel structure started to wobble and collapse.

"Ohmygosh!" Molly shrieked. "I don't believe it! That's Lea and Bobby Langster from school! We can't leave 'em there! Get us closer!"

The Skeleton swung the pumpkin balloon around, sailing toward disaster. A surge of flame bolted from the girl's hand, sizzling on impact, but the monster barely flinched. It had blindly groped its way before, but suddenly, sickeningly, a vast multitude of baleful black eyes burst open on the pulsing pseudo-pods. A hungry tendril whipped its way toward those screaming on the Ferris Wheel.

Heh Heh Heh Heh Heh Heh Heh Heh Heh!!

A swift grey shape shot past them like an arrow, cackling like a banshee. Molly rubbed her eyes, and looked again. Then, again. She still could hardly believe it. The phantom streaked across the crescent face of the moon, and then darted down toward them again.

Flying astride her broomstick, the Witch rocketed at the squirming abomination. In her left hand she held aloft a gleaming green globe, took aim, and let it go. Night became day, the air suddenly loud with light. It's thousand eyes blinded, the monster lurched, releasing the Ferris Wheel.

Towering tentacles flailed madly, the awful thing roaring in rage. Molly delivered another volley of flame. The Skeleton wrestled against the whip-like fury. Autumn glowered, snarling a sound most un-catlike.

Abruptly, the cephalopod colossus ceased to be. In the blink of an eye, it crumbled into a fine grey ash mixing with a swirling flock of oak leaves.

Freddy appeared, hovering above Lea and Bobby.

"Wh-what's that?" Bobby stammered. "Whaddaya call that, sis? Huh?"

"Uh, hi there," the Ghost greeted them. "I'm suppose to tell ya not to be skeered. It's all part of th' show!"

His wispy shape solidified into something like a luminous jellyfish.

"Grab on!" he directed.

Bobby wouldn't move until his sister took the lead.

"What have we got to lose?" she giggled.

"It's a ghost!" Bobby screeched.

"Don't be goofy. No such thing. C'mon, this'll be fun!"

Slowly, almost lazily, Freddy floated the teenagers safely to the ground.

The Witch did a loop on the broomstick and plummeted toward the balloon, snatching Molly from the basket and into the sky. The girl yelped, dizzy and dazzled. Far below, a cautious round of clapping littered the crowd, quickly swelling into thunderous applause.

The girl shook her head.

"I don't believe it!" she shouted above the rushing wind. "Everyone thinks this was all fake—like some kinda big corny magic show!"

"Hold on tight, child! Show's not over yet!" the grey lady laughed. "Next stop— Bee Knob Hill!"

BEE KNOB Hill, at midnight, was as solemn and sinister as it gets.

"How'd you ever find this creepy place?" Molly shivered.

Miss Grimalkin plucked an oak leaf from her pouch, then let it flutter to the ground.

"The leaves of trees make excellent spies," she explained. "They scurry about everywhere, hear everything, and nobody ever notices. You just need to know how to listen to them. Fortunately, I'm fluent in oak, willow, birch, and a number of others. It might have taken weeks for us to search this hill top for the Phooka, otherwise."

"Jeepers... flying broomsticks, talking to leaves... " the girl smiled. "You really are a crazy ol' witch, aren'tcha?"

The grey lady grinned back.

"The witchiest. Now, come along, dear. Let's find our Phooka."

They hiked for several minutes in silence before Miss Grimalkin stopped and pointed. Molly's eyes grew wide.

"We're here."

It was a dead place, as dead as could be imagined. No crickets, no other bugs nor even bats. An abandoned ancient school bus lay on its side, half swallowed in the earth. Gnarled trees twisted around its rusty shell in torment, lifeless and still. Not even a breeze dared stir there.

"This is called 'Buzzard's Roost," the grey lady whispered. "Nobody ever comes here. It's the perfect place to hide."

Molly gulped.

"You mean it... it's in that old bus?"

"Has to be," the Witch nodded. "I'll go first, and you follow."

The back bus door was stubborn with age, but the grey lady soon had it open, creaking from its crusted hinges. She removed her tall peaked hat, poking her head inside the yawning entry.

"It's all right, child," the Witch said sadly. "Come say hello."

The girl bit her lip again, and crept forward on shaky knees. Peering over the Witch's shoulder, her eyes brimmed with tears.

Within the dusty old bus, still and silent in a pale moonbeam, lay a web-veiled pile of yellowed bones with a regal horned skull.

"I don't understand," Molly sobbed.

"Autumn had already surmised most of this mystery," Miss Grimalkin replied. "The Phooka used this place as its lair. Look there on the ceiling... "

Molly's finger flickered with bright flame illuminating the spot.

"The metal looks scorched," she mused. "Kinda melted."

"Struck by lightning," the grey lady nodded. "The Phooka died in its sleep... as it lay dreaming. Its dreams, somehow, lived on, and its nightmares, too."

"I think I get it now," Molly said softly. "That's why the creatures it conjured crumbled in the daylight, like all bad dreams."

"And that's why my sun-sphere, a potion that takes a whole week to brew, finally did the job at the carnival," the Witch added, worriedly. Phookas are so rare, much remains unknown about them. The fact that the poor thing came to this area is troublesome."

Molly glanced from the silent bones to the grey lady.

"You mean because of them being 'heralds of doom', like you said?"

"Exactly, child," she put a comforting arm around the girl's shoulders. "Perhaps we should stay in Woodland for a while longer, before moving on. Just to be sure."

A hot tear streaked Molly's cheek.

"I wish I'd seen it alive."

The Witch cupped the girl's chin.

"We're not done here," she explained. "The spell's not broken yet. The Phooka cannot awake. It will dream again, creating more living nightmares."

"What can we do?"

"Its earthly remains must be obliterated. A good hot fire will do it."

Molly understood, embers already smoldering in her eyes.

"Rest in peace, Phooka," she whispered. "No more bad dreams."

WHEN THEY arrived back at the carnival, the crowds had gone. Autumn the black cat was curled upon the ectoplasmic lap of Freddy the Ghost, quite comfortable with each other, as they watched the eager clean-up crew. Thurston and his rag-men were in a flurry, sweeping up heaping mounds of the dead grey dust. One hundred-per-cent efficiently, of course.

The Skeleton had moored the pumpkin balloon to the base of the Ferris Wheel, standing alone, lost in solitary thought as was his custom. He struck an impressive, powerfully chiseled figure there in the moonlight. Molly immediately walked over to him as Miss Grimalkin conferred with Sheriff Les.

"You were right," he admitted, worn and tired. "About everything. It's like a cyclone has hit the countryside. Practically every farm sustained some damage, but it's a lot worse in town. Vine Grove looks like it's been stomped to the ground by a giant boot. My missus's restaurant is a pile of rubble. The weather guys are blamin' it all on a freak wind storm. They don't know what else to call it. Y'know, an awful lot of folks wouldn't be alive right now, if they hadn't been there at your carnival. Thanks… thank you for that."

"Why Sheriff!" the Witch exclaimed. "Almost sounds like you're starting to trust us!"

"YOU OKAY?" Molly shyly approached the Skeleton.

"Are you?" his piercing eyes lost some of their edge.

"Sure. I'm just peachy. So, I've been meaning to ask you… does that laboratory gizmo of yours play all the TV stations?"

"It does."

"Well, y'know… there's a monster movie marathon on Channel 41. Wanna watch it with me?"

"I don't think so."

"S'matter?" she grinned. "Too scary for you?"

The half-smile starting to play beneath the skull mask was cut short by a deafening explosion. And the Skeleton dropped.

Trooper Dick Ashcraft, perspiring and pale, stood there with his shotgun smoking.

EPILOGUE

"I'M SO sorry," Sheriff Les said.

Miss Grimalkin escorted him to his squad car.

"Not your fault, my boy," she patted his shoulder. "Not even Autumn saw it coming."

Les grimaced.

"Ashcraft always was half off his rocker. Guess tonight just ran 'im pure crazy. We got 'im locked up in down in Sandridge Sanitarium. He's howlin' 'bout how he saved the town from monsters. Doubt they'll ever let 'im out. Won't be botherin' you again, anyway. I saw the girl outside by his grave. Guess she's still takin' it pretty hard."

"They understood each other, Sheriff," the Witch replied. "A rare thing in this world. That sort of thing doesn't ever die."

MOLLY KNELT by the mound. A stick-mounted skull mask swayed gently near the nameless headstone. The black cat kept her company. Gigantic Jack O' Lantern searchlights blazed the soot-colored sky in honor of their fallen friend.

"It's not fair, Autumn," the girl somberly said. "We were just getting to know each other. He seemed so sad and lonely. I only wanted to make him laugh."

A cold drizzle started to fall and Molly turned to leave. A low, odd noise from Autumn stopped her.

"S'matter, cat? Did I forget someth—OHMYGOODNESS!"

Quickly, soundlessly, the costumed giant rose from beneath the black earth.

Molly stood and stared, stunned into silence. The Skeleton staggered and stretched, and then dusted himself off. Grabbing the mask, he quickly drew it over his great head.

"But..." Molly muttered, "...but... b-but..."

"Surprised?" he asked in his familiar baritone. "I told you I had a single magic power. And yes. It hurts."

"You... you mean... you can come back from the dead?" she asked, utterly astonished.

"Well, so far."

The girl timidly poked him with a nervous finger. The black cat yawned.

"You're not a ghost like Freddy, anyways. Wowza..."

"Let's get out of the rain," he suggested.

Giant, girl, and cat headed back toward the carnival.

"I saw your real face, y'know," Molly trotted to keep up.

"Yes."

"Don't worry, you're not so bad without the mask."

"Oh?"

"Nah. I could hardly tell the difference."

"Very funny."

"Sure you weren't wearing another mask under that one?"

" Hmph."

"See? Didja see? I knew it! I knew I could make you smile. Y'know, there's something I haven't said since I was a real little kid, and I kinda wanna say right now because I feel like, for the first time, I really mean it."

"Oh? What's that?"

"Happy Halloween."

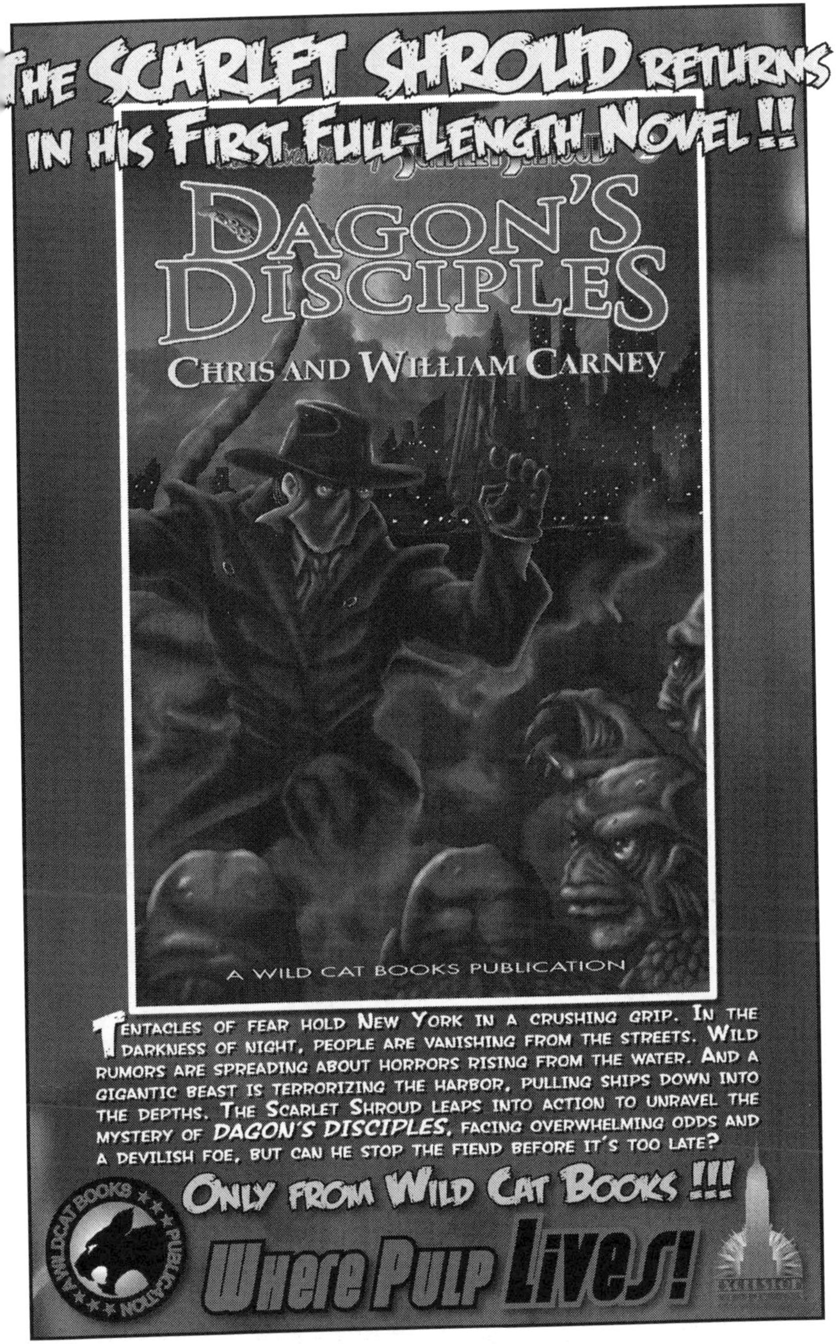